WHEN ANNA CAME HOME

Shannon Condon

First published 2025
by Rowanvale Books Ltd
The Gate
Keppoch Street
Roath
Cardiff
CF24 3JW
www.rowanvalebooks.com

A CIP catalogue record for this book is available from the British Library.
ISBN: 978-1-83584-039-9
eBook ISBN: 978-1-83584-040-5

This book is dedicated to my mother. Thank you for listening to my story ideas before your morning coffee, encouraging me to follow my dreams and always believing in me.

"The eye sees only what the mind is prepared to comprehend."

– Robertson Davies

CHAPTER 1

October 1, 2016

The new moon shrouded the cargo area of Savannah International Airport in darkness. The only illumination was the light poking through the bottom of the closed hangar door. Inside, four men dressed in black were loading a dozen sealed crates into a commercial freight carrier.

As they worked diligently and quietly, a man in his fifties stood off to the side, overseeing the operation.

"Lieutenant Colonel." One of the workers walked up to him and saluted.

"Dammit, son. Don't salute me and don't call me that—you might as well be shouting out my name."

"I apologize, sir. The lookout radioed. A black sedan just pulled up next to the side door."

"It's about damn time!"

The officer walked outside to find a younger man unloading two duffel bags from the car. He bent down to unzip the bags, while the latter stood uncomfortably in the light spilling from his trunk.

"There is five million dollars between the two bags. I was instructed to tell you the rest will be delivered once the cargo reaches its destination."

"Good. You can go now. Keep your headlights off until you are through the gates and on the access road."

The man closed his trunk and grabbed the officer's arm before he could walk away. The older man turned with an angry glare, but he held his ground.

"I want my cut. We agreed on a quarter of a million dollars."

The officer dropped one of the bags and pulled out two stacks of bills—one hundred thousand dollars. "You'll get the rest when I get mine. Now, go!"

Irritated, the younger man got back in his car and drove away. The officer loaded the duffels into his own car, parked at the rear of the hangar, then went back inside. The cargo had been stacked and tied down to keep the crates from sliding during takeoff and landing. Two pilots approached him to review the manifest.

"We have twelve crates to be delivered to these coordinates in Doha, Qatar. Would you confirm, please?"

He pulled out his phone and checked the location of the runway in Doha. He nodded as he returned the manifest. "Your location is correct. Are you sure you have enough fuel for no stops en route?"

"Yes, sir. I weighed the cargo; it's light compared to our usual load. There won't be any need for refueling," the pilot assured him.

The officer waved for two of his men to enter the cargo hold. Each had an automatic rifle. "These boys will make sure there's no trouble and the shipment reaches its destination on time."

"What about our payment?" the pilot asked.

"You'll be paid upon delivery in Doha. Get moving. These people don't like to wait."

The cargo door on the plane closed and the hangar door opened, allowing the freight carrier to taxi down the runway and take off into the night. The lights in the hangar were shut off, and the officer and his remaining men exited out the back, where the lookout was waiting for them.

The officer opened his trunk and handed each of the soldiers fifty thousand dollars, looking each one dead in the eye. Without saying a word, they understood. If they opened their mouths, they'd be as dead as the two pilots when they reached Doha.

In the darkness, the cars left the airport and headed back to base.

CHAPTER 2

March 10, 2017

As Anna walked through the open door, her stomach lurched in warning. Her hand flew to her mouth.

"Bathroom is the first one on the left." Special Agent Mallory pointed her toward the correct door.

Anna got there just in time. Her petite body convulsed for fifteen torturous minutes until even the bile was gone. When she finally sat back, she noticed the marble flooring—this was a hotel bathroom. *Why am I here? Why not at the FBI field office?*

She didn't have time to wonder further before Special Agent Kate DeSoto knocked at the door. Kate peered in at Anna, shaking on the cold floor.

"Come on, Anna. Let's get you to the sink and clean you up."

Anna didn't realize how wobbly she had become. Her first try at standing almost brought them both down. Kate, though not much bigger than Anna, had the strength of an average man and then some. She stood five foot five inches tall and had short black hair. Though she had recently turned thirty, the long hours and nature of her work belied her youth.

While Anna held on to the sink, Kate grabbed a clean shirt and the toiletry bag from Anna's suitcase. The special agent gave Anna privacy as she took off her vomit-stained Ohio State University sweatshirt and replaced it with a green Henley.

Anna brushed her teeth and took the opportunity to look at herself in the mirror. She looked as bad as she felt. Her golden blonde hair was half out of its ponytail, and her pale blue eyes were swollen from the tears she'd cried and the ones still waiting to be shed. She tried her best to neaten up her hair and fished some acetaminophen out of her bag.

When she opened the bathroom door, Kate was waiting to escort her to the sitting area and SA Mallory, who was waiting patiently.

"Why am I in a hotel suite and not at the FBI office?" Anna asked him.

Mike sighed, and Anna could see sympathy in his eyes. "No one knows there was a witness to the shootings today. We need to keep it that way until we get your statement and can ensure your safety."

The events of the day flooded her mind. She hadn't forgotten them; her brain was just overloaded, and she had been able to close that door for a blessed moment. Now it was wide open.

"Oh my God! My family, they were all shot," she whispered, afraid to say it out loud, as if that would make it real.

"Oliver is in the hospital. We don't know about his condition yet. I'm sorry. We will let you know as soon as we get an update."

The bullet that struck Oliver had torn through his femoral artery and he'd lost a large amount of blood. He was undergoing surgery at Evanston Hospital. Mike kept that to himself. Right now, he needed to get a statement from his only witness before she went down the rabbit hole of grief.

He hadn't said anything about her three other family members. The omission told Anna enough—they had not survived. She ran back to the bathroom and vomited out the acetaminophen and water she had just drunk.

Kate wet a washcloth and wiped Anna's face. She was motherly in her touch and spoke quietly, trying to calm and encourage her at the same time. "Anna, the best thing you can do for your family right now is give us a recorded account of what you saw."

Anna stood and tried to steady her breath. Kate led her back into the main room.

"What do you need me to do?" Anna asked quietly.

Mike Mallory was a large man who, five years from retirement, had witnessed enough violence in the Chicagoland area to last a lifetime. Gray hair and dark circles under his eyes made him look older than his fifty-seven years.

"Anna. I'm going to have you sit in that chair and I'll be taking a video statement with my iPhone. Answer my questions to the best of your ability. I'll try to make this as quick as possible, but it's important you give us as much detail as you can."

Anna nodded and went to sit in the black chair against the white wall. Her heart was pounding in her chest at the thought of what she was about to recount and the consequences of it.

"Please state your full name and age." Mike started the questioning.

"Anna Grace Cahill. I'm twenty-two years old."

"Anna, was your family expecting you to arrive at home in Winnetka today?"

"No. My original plan was to fly to Aruba with a few of my friends for spring break."

"Did anyone know you were arriving in Winnetka today?"

"Yes, the friends I was supposed to go with to Aruba."

"What changed your plans? In detail please."

"About two weeks ago, I received my acceptance letter to Northwestern University Pritzker School of Law. I never told my parents I was applying. I wanted to come home and tell them in person."

"What time did you arrive home?"

"The car service dropped me off at about one-thirty p.m."

"Did anyone see you enter the house?"

"No. When the car dropped me off, I noticed my brother Oliver and my uncle David's cars were in the driveway. If they were meeting with my father at our house on a workday, I assumed it would be important and private. I didn't want to interrupt so I went to the side door, let myself in and went up the back stairway to my bedroom."

"What is your family's business?"

"Cahill Investment Bankers. My great-grandfather started it after World War II. The office is located on Adams Street in downtown Chicago."

"What occurred next?"

Anna closed her eyes, trying to hold back the hot tears threatening to erupt. Her fingernails dug into her palms.

Kate cut into the conversation. "Anna, would you like to take a few minutes to collect yourself before we move on?"

Mike stopped recording.

Relief flooded Anna's body, untangling her muscles as it moved its way from her shoulders to her feet. Kate handed her a ginger ale from the minibar.

"I have a prescription for anxiety in my backpack. May I take it before we continue?" Anna looked hopefully between them.

"I'm sorry, Anna." Kate responded first. "You can't be under the influence of any sedatives when you give your statement. Once we finish, you can take your medication."

Anna slumped in her chair and nodded her understanding. She took a few sips of the ginger ale, followed by several deep breaths.

She looked at Mike behind the camera. "Okay. Let's continue."

Mike resumed recording. "Anna, you said you went up the back stairs to your room. Are you sure no one saw you?"

"Yes. The side door opens into the kitchen, which was empty. The stairs are right inside the door. I was able to go directly up to my room without anyone seeing me."

"What occurred next? In as much detail as you remember."

"I heard loud voices coming from downstairs. We have a large circular foyer on the first floor, which is marble. The main staircase is in the foyer and leads upstairs to a decorative balcony that's also marble, with columns and a wrought iron railing. The hard surfaces make any noise downstairs resonate. Three loud popping sounds startled me. I crawled down the hall to the balcony and hid behind a column to see what was going on. My family was in the study with the doors open."

"Please state for the record who was in the study. First and last names."

"My parents, Thomas and Meredith Cahill; my brother, Oliver Cahill; my uncle, David Cahill, and a man I didn't recognize."

"What did you see when you looked in the study?"

Anna tried to take a deep breath, but her lungs rebelled. She looked at Mike's face above the camera and was met with a set stare.

"Keep going, Anna. You can do it," he told her.

She glanced at Kate, who nodded encouragingly.

Anna grabbed the sides of her chair, closed her eyes and rocked back and forth. When she opened her eyes, words tumbled out of her mouth uncontrollably as tears poured from her eyes.

"My mom, dad and uncle were lying on the floor. They had been shot. I saw Oliver jump on the man with the gun, knocking him to the floor. They were wrestling and yelling at each other. I heard two more loud popping sounds. The man rolled off Oliver and lay on the floor. He had his back to me, but I could see blood pooling around him. I looked at Oliver. He was on his back and there was a large amount of blood running from his thigh. There was blood everywhere. I was terrified. I crawled back to my room, hid in the closet and called you. You told me you were contacting emergency services. I heard the sirens but I was still too afraid to come out. Then you and SA DeSoto came and got me."

"Could you hear what your brother and the man were arguing about?"

Anna shook her head, defeated. "My ears were ringing."

"Did you see the man's face?"

"No, he had his back to me. Everything happened so fast."

"Can you tell me his height or hair color? What was he wearing?" Mike pushed.

"I was looking down on them so I'm not sure how tall he was, but he was shorter than Oliver, and he's six feet tall. The man was wearing jeans and a black jacket. He was bald and had a jagged scar on the back of his head. Is he dead too? Who is he? Why did he do this to my family?"

Mike stopped recording. "I don't have all the answers now, Anna. I promise you I'll find out who was behind this. You've been very helpful," he tried to reassure her.

Kate held back tears as she watched Anna fold in on herself in the chair with a banshee's wail, as if she could scream the pain out of her. Mike directed Kate to get Anna her prescription bottle.

Anna quickly grabbed two anxiety pills and swallowed them with the ginger ale. Soon she was on the sofa, curled up in a ball, crying as she again rocked back and forth, waiting for the numbness to come.

Mike left to rush the taped statement to his supervisor. The special agents had brought Anna to the hotel without authorization, and he needed to get ahead of the blowback. Right now, the two of them were the only ones who knew there was an eyewitness. And she was a Cahill; Anna needed to be in a safe house, and a discussion with Oliver Cahill was critical.

Mike and Kate had been less than seventy-two hours from raiding Cahill Investment Bankers. Now he didn't know what would happen.

Because of Anna's call, the FBI had arrived just after the local police. Mike explained to the lead officer that the victims had been under federal investigation. The FBI had been allowed to commandeer the scene, and the locals blocked the road so no news trucks could get through.

If details of this crime hit the evening news, nine months and hundreds of hours of work would evaporate.

CHAPTER 3

December 16, 2016

Anna's eyes feasted on her parents' pantry. She was still acclimating, coming off the final week of the semester having gone for several papers and presentations with little food and even less sleep. As she loaded her arms with peanut butter, bread and chips, she heard a familiar voice calling her name in the cavernous foyer. She laid her spread on the kitchen island and waited for him to come find her.

The excitement built in her; she felt like a child waiting for a parent to come home. Oliver was her older brother by seven years, and she idolized him. Her smile reached from ear to ear as he strolled across the marble entrance hall and into the kitchen. He was six foot tall, with broad shoulders, green eyes and wavy chestnut hair. He snatched her up and spun her around.

"Hey Peanut!" He laughed. "You're looking a little rough today." Oliver put her down and sat on the stool at the island.

Anna teasingly smacked the back of his head while he dug into the bag of chips. "Careful, you'll get grease all over your Armani sweater," she said. "Why did it take this long to come and see me?"

"Sorry, work has been insane. Seriously." He looked at her. "How did your finals go?"

Anna made them both peanut butter sandwiches. "Good, I think. No exams, just papers and presentations. The last few weeks have been a blur. My grades should be posted early next week."

As she handed him his plate, Oliver leaned forward, asking in a conspiratorial tone, "Should we make our usual wager?"

Anna felt the laughter bubbling up inside her until it overflowed. It felt good to laugh after the intensity of the past semester.

"Yup. Twenty bucks. I say within fifteen minutes." Anna gave a mischievous smile.

"Wow, you are harsh! I'm giving Mom the benefit of the doubt. Thirty minutes."

Anna launched into her sandwich, and she and Oliver drank their Cokes and caught up on gossip. Apparently, at the tender age of twenty-nine, he was considered one of the most eligible bachelors in Chicago. Anna rolled her eyes dramatically. *As if his ego needed more feeding.*

Oliver leaned towards her and whispered, "Did you get your LSAT scores yet?"

Anna looked around to make sure her mother wasn't in earshot, then back at her brother. "Yes, but it's a secret. Don't ask me here!"

"No one is listening, Ms. CIA," Oliver prodded. "Give me the number."

Anna sighed but whispered back, "One hundred seventy."

Oliver stood up and pumped his fists in the air. "Amazing! I knew you could do it!"

"Sit down!" she exclaimed, but she couldn't hide her smile.

"Where did you apply?"

"OSU, of course. DePaul, Loyola and Northwestern."

Oliver grinned, gave her a high five and then ate half his sandwich in two bites.

"Manners, much?" Anna asked, chuckling.

They both were laughing when Meredith Cahill glided into the kitchen. At fifty-eight, she was stunning. She shared the same hair color as her son, but her waves were tamed into a stylish bob ending just below her chin. Meredith stood five foot six inches but always wore at least a three-inch heel, accentuating her lithe figure. Anna looked at her mom with admiration. She exuded elegance without effort.

"Oliver, I wasn't expecting you tonight. What a nice surprise!" Meredith kissed her son on the head.

"I came to kidnap Anna," Oliver joked. "I need her help with my Christmas shopping so I thought she could stay at my place in the city tonight and we can hit the Magnificent Mile tomorrow."

"Yes!" Anna jumped up. "Mom, would you mind? I need to do my shopping too. I didn't have time with finals."

She knew Oliver had an ulterior motive—he always did—but seeing the city in all its Christmas splendor would be so much fun.

Meredith pursed her lips for a moment, and Anna felt her stomach start to sink. Her mother usually wanted her to stay in Winnetka when she came home from college.

"You just got home on Sunday, and the company Christmas party is tomorrow night at The Peninsula. I booked us a suite so we can get ready together."

"I'll make sure she is at the hotel by three o'clock tomorrow," Oliver said with his winning grin.

Anna knew her mom was sold. She rarely said no to him.

"Fine." She turned to Anna. "Make sure you try on the dress I bought you before you leave tonight. It's hanging in your closet. If you've gained any weight, it won't fit." Meredith gestured to the peanut butter sandwich in Anna's hand.

"Oliver is eating the same thing," Anna replied defensively.

"Yes, but he has an excellent metabolism, like me," she said gently as she gestured to her slim silhouette. "We don't know about yours. You stopped cheering at OSU after sophomore year. Do you know how many girls would kill to be a college cheerleader?"

Anna shrank on her stool, listening to the usual barb. "Mom, I told you it was interfering with my academics." She tried to hide her frustration.

"That's just poor time management," Meredith chided before she kissed her daughter's head. "Don't worry, we'll keep you on track over the holidays. You're too pretty to be overweight."

Anna smiled and threw the rest of her sandwich in the garbage.

"Thanks, Mom. I'll go try on that dress and grab my suitcase."

"That's my girl." Meredith gave Anna a warm squeeze. "Oh, try on the new black heels I picked up for you. You should wear heels more often." She winked and headed toward the study, her own heels clacking on the marble floor.

Anna looked at Oliver and mouthed, "Twenty bucks!" before she ran up the back stairs.

***

Anna held her breath as she saw her reflection in the full-length mirror. The dress her mother had picked out was beyond elegant: midnight blue silk with a neckline barely skimming her shoulders, draped just low enough to show her slender neck and collarbone. Among the folds of the draping were Swarovski crystals, matching the ones along the bottom of the three-quarter length trumpet sleeves. The body of the dress was a sheath ending just above her knees. The fit was perfect, not too tight nor too loose.

She couldn't help but laugh when she noticed the shoes her mom had bought. Louboutin pumps that cost ten times more than she would ever spend herself.

As Anna stood in front of the mirror, she felt beautiful. For a moment. Then her mother's words about her weight started echoing in her head and Anna felt the familiar tightness start in her chest. She quickly slipped the dress off and carefully placed it back in the hanging bag along with the black pumps. She took one of her anxiety pills. She didn't want to be in a full-blown panic attack on the way into the city.

Anna sat on the bed and took a moment. She owed a lot to her mom. How many of her friends had told her she'd won the lottery when she was adopted into the Cahill family? Her mom was always affectionate and loving towards her, but she was controlling. Anna had started dance lessons at age four, gymnastics at seven and cheerleading by ten. Meredith had kept a diary of her weight and measurements from the time she was twelve years old.

Her father, however, rarely mustered any acknowledgment of his only daughter. She'd learned early on to tread lightly when he was around. Thomas Cahill made no secret her adoption was not something he'd wanted. He already had two sons, Tommy and Oliver. They were his legacy.

Anna felt a shiver down her spine as she recalled the night Oliver told her about Tommy. His brother had been eight, riding his bike home from a neighbor's house, just in time for dinner. It was fall and dusk was coming earlier. One block from home, a drunk driver ran a stop sign and hit him at forty miles per hour. Tommy died on impact. Meredith had heard the crash and with a mother's instinct flew out of the front door. She cradled her son until the police pulled her away. Five-year-old Oliver watched from the lawn, forgotten in the turmoil. Anna had cried for him when he first told her about Tommy's death.

As devastated as his mother was, his father's grief was particularly acute. He spent more time at work and withdrew from everyone.

Two years later, thanks to Meredith's determination and despite Thomas' disapproval, they adopted an infant girl. Anna. Oliver had told her she'd lifted the dark veil that'd hung over them since Tommy's death.

Anna's counselor at the university told her this was where her anxiety first stemmed from. She loved Oliver and her mom and never wanted to disappoint them, often to her own detriment.

Anna smoothed the fabric of her new dress before zipping up the bag. She smiled, knowing her mother had picked it out especially for her.

CHAPTER 4

December 16, 2016

"I can't believe this view you have, Oliver! I can see all the way to Lake Michigan, even though it's a black blob right now," Anna said with a laugh.

Oliver smiled at her. She was standing with her back to him, looking out the wall of windows that was the main feature of his penthouse apartment. He was pouring her a glass of wine, mulling over the news he was about to give her. His sister was an innocent, but he was in a serious bind and Anna would never let him down.

"Here you go, Annie." He walked over to the coffee table and set down her glass of Riesling, flipping on the fireplace as he passed it.

"You know I hate it when you call me that." Anna screwed up her face as she fell onto the cushy sofa and grabbed her wine.

"That's why I do it." Oliver laughed. "Ok, I'm going to order us dinner and then we can catch up."

"Make it something healthy," Anna said, savoring her first sip.

"Absolutely not. I'm ordering our favorite Chinese, and you are going to eat every bit of it. I won't let Mom get in your head. There's nothing wrong with your weight. You need to stop letting her dictate your every move." Oliver took out his phone, making sure Anna saw him ordering her favorite dishes.

"She's not that bad," she countered.

"You'd be surprised," Oliver responded with a side glance. He drained his glass of whisky and got up to pour another.

"Something's up if you are hitting the Macallan this early."

Oliver could hear the concern in his sister's voice but deflected for now. "Anna, tell me why you never told Mom and Dad you took the LSATs."

"You know why, Oliver."

"I want you to tell me," he insisted.

He could see her frustration, but he wanted her to say it out loud. Something she had never openly admitted.

Anna leaned back against the sofa. Exasperated, she said, "First of all, Dad couldn't care less what I do. He barely acknowledges my existence. Secondly, Mom is an amazing lawyer, and if I bombed my LSATs or if I can't get into a good law school, I don't want to embarrass her."

"What if I told you she's not so amazing? She could be disbarred for some of the things she's done." Oliver watched his sister closely.

"I'm not sure what you are alluding to, but I know you didn't invite me here to go Christmas shopping. So, spill."

"You might want some of this first." Oliver raised his Macallan with a smile, in a desperate attempt to lighten the mood. Anna's glare told him to start talking.

"Let's eat first," he said instead. "The food will be here soon. You may not feel like eating after I tell you everything."

Anna stared as he poured another Scotch.

***

"It started when I passed my Series 79 exam four years ago. Dad moved me up to the Mergers and Acquisitions department. I worked with Uncle David on client files he categorized as the 'big fish' for our firm. They were buyers who wanted to acquire large corporations. For each client, I would do the research, present David with possible acquisitions and then perform due diligence on the corporation our client chose. I presented a financial report and buyout recommendation. David would negotiate on behalf of our client. Many of these clients wanted to acquire more than one corporation in different industries.

"About eighteen months ago, David gave me a few of the big clients to handle on my own. By this time, I was already neck deep in so many of their acquisitions. Once I saw the full files, I realized our clients were shell companies, hiding the identities of the real buyers. My first shock came when I saw who set up the shells: Meredith Cahill, Esquire."

Oliver watched in discomfort as his sister's eyes narrowed and her beautiful blue irises darkened. She was not a finance major, but growing up around the family business, her instincts were strong. Still, he continued.

"I came to the house on a weekend I knew Mom and Dad would both be out of town. I went through Mom's office—she would never keep those files at her firm. I found the flash drive in her wall safe."

"How did you know the combination?" Anna was leaning closer, barely breathing.

"Tommy's birthday. It was a no-brainer. I downloaded the files onto my laptop, replaced the flash drive and left. When I got back home, I read through every file. Each shell company was funded by a foreign company or specially designated national on OFAC's blacklist. We're helping terrorists, arms dealers, drug dealers, you name it, buy American companies. Mom, Dad, Uncle David, they're all in on it, and now I'm involved too."

"But you didn't know," Anna said defensively.

"It doesn't matter. My name is all over those files. I'm totally fucked, Anna!"

"Why didn't you quit when you discovered all of this?"

"I tried. I went to Dad and Uncle David." Oliver struggled to hold back tears. "They doctored the files, removed their names from every document. They set me up."

Anna stood up and started pacing the length of the room. A steady stream of swear words was escaping under her breath. "I can't believe Mom would do something illegal like that. She loves the law."

"But she is afraid of Dad, and fear is a much stronger emotion." He could see that this was a hard pill for Anna to swallow.

"Even if Dad made her set up the shell companies, Mom loves you. I know she wouldn't throw you to the wolves like that!" Anna was vehement.

"To be fair, she didn't know Dad and David were going to involve me." Oliver's voice was louder than he intended.

"Still, Mom would have found a way to clear you. She'd never let them implicate you."

"Well, she did! I have undeniable proof. You know firsthand how cruel our father can be if you cross him!" He was shouting now.

"Is that how you paid for this condo? It must have cost a fortune." Anna eyed him with suspicion.

"No, I used the inheritance from Grandpa Cahill. You got the same thing," Oliver replied, indignant.

"Really? This is the first I'm hearing about a lot of things!" Anna stood facing him with her hands on her hips.

"He gave us both an equal inheritance. Before he died, he set up a Uniform Transfer to Minors Act account for each of us in the amount of a million dollars to be received when we reached twenty-one years of age. Dad was appointed custodian of the accounts."

Oliver stared at Anna's confused face, and then he realized. "Holy shit! Dad never told you."

Anna's bewildered look quickly turned to a scowl. "No, he never mentioned it. Son of a bitch! By law, I should have received it last year. I think I've got some digging to do in his study."

"Don't risk going in there. You know what happened last time you went where you weren't allowed." Anna flinched involuntarily at the memory. "I still have a copy of the attorney's letter. You can go into the bank yourself and transfer it to a new account. I would strongly suggest you move the money that's in the account to an offshore bank as soon as possible."

"Why would I do that?"

"Because the FBI will freeze all our assets, and yours might be frozen too, even if you aren't part of the company. Move it to where it can't be found."

"The FBI?" Anna was slack-jawed.

"I was approached on Monday by two FBI special agents. The Department of Justice is investigating Cahill Investment Bankers. They didn't give me details, but they seemed to believe what I told them and offered me immunity if I gather information for them."

"Tell me you agreed."

"That's why I brought you here, Anna. You're my alibi for tomorrow. I'm going to meet with them and go over the details while my driver takes you to Michigan Avenue for Christmas shopping."

"Can I come with you? I'll be in the house for the next few weeks. I'll have plenty of opportunities to gather information for you to give the FBI."

Oliver hugged his sister. "I wish you could, but any deal would be off the table if the special agents knew I had told someone. My future is on the line."

He could see in her eyes she was disappointed, but she nodded her understanding.

"What about Mom? Do you think you can get them to go easy on her?"

"I don't know. I'm not in a position to ask for favors. I'll let them know Dad coerced her. I'm not sure if it will help or not. Legally, she should have reported Dad as soon as she knew. You know that as well as I do."

Anna leaned her head back on the sofa and covered her eyes, but she couldn't stave off the tears. How was she supposed to face her parents tomorrow?

"Maybe I should start looking for my biological parents," she said wistfully.

CHAPTER 5

December 17, 2016

Oliver stared out over the dark Chicago skyline. He'd needed an alibi, desperately—getting Anna involved was his only option. He'd told her about the FBI investigation but omitted most of the story.

He was already in neck-deep with the FBI. The meeting today was with his "handlers" and the chief federal prosecutor.

Oliver had driven to a safe house in the northwest suburb of Schaumburg. Dressed in jeans, a sweater and peacoat, carrying an Aldi grocery bag containing evidence, he knocked on the side door of a brick house in a middle-class neighborhood.

Special Agents Mallory and DeSoto ushered him into the mudroom, and Mike quickly patted him down, checking for any weapons or wires. Kate rifled through the contents of the bag. Satisfied, they led him to the family room, where the sheer drapes were closed, and had him sit on the sofa. Oliver slid out of his coat and laid it beside him.

"Coffee?" asked Kate.

"No, thank you."

He could feel the sweat pooling under his armpits, even though it was below freezing outside and the heat didn't seem to be turned on in the house. His attorney had been very specific with his instructions. Oliver wasn't to turn over any evidence until he saw a signed letter by the chief prosecutor giving him full immunity. He'd already put himself at risk by verbally sharing information with the special agents.

The slam of the side door made all three occupants jump. Oliver stood as a man in his fifties, portly with a ring of hair around his head, walked in and wordlessly commanded everyone's attention.

"Oliver Cahill?"

Oliver nodded as the man's meaty hand took his and shook it firmly.

"I'm Chief Federal Prosecutor Greg Kirkland." He motioned for all of them to sit down. "So, Kate and Mike tell me you have some valuable information that will help us."

"Yes, sir."

"Well, I haven't got all day. I have a plane to catch back to D.C. Show me what you have." Kirkland's voice was friendly but had a razor's edge beneath it.

"I believe you have something to show me first, Mr. Kirkland," Oliver said calmly, but inside, his heart was threatening to break free of his sweater.

Kirkland laughed, a caustic snort. Kate and Mike exchanged concerned looks.

"No good deed is without its price—right, Oliver?" Kirkland reached into his suit pocket and pulled out a folded letter. He laid it out on the table for Oliver to read.

It was his letter of immunity. When Oliver went to pick it up, Kirkland snatched it back.

"Sorry, I can't have you carrying around a 'get out of jail free' letter from the federal government. Call your attorney. He will confirm he has a copy for safekeeping."

Oliver pulled out his phone and dialed. The conversation was brief. They had a copy. He was safe.

He spent the next thirty minutes explaining the evidence he'd provided. When Mike questioned why he had risked bringing paper files, Oliver gave him a brief background on their system.

"These files are kept on the main network and are password protected. All the assistants have the same password so they can print documents for their bosses. However, they can't download anything. Only the owner of the file can download or edit these documents. I would've had to enter my code to put this on a flash drive. It was safest to use the assistant code to print them. The flash drive I am giving you is information I pulled from my mother's computer. It contains all the shell companies created and their actual owners through the end of October."

"Smart move, Oliver," Kate remarked.

Kirkland let out a low growl of discontent.

"Listen, I'm on your side," Oliver said quickly. "As I told you when we first spoke, my dad and uncle screwed me over. I had no idea they were helping terrorists and arms dealers buy American companies. I didn't realize they were framing me. Just tell me what else you need, and I will get it for you."

Kirkland was sitting in the chair diagonal from Oliver. He leaned forward with his elbows on his knees and dropped his voice. Even the two special agents had to slide in to hear.

"Oliver, there is a known benefactor of a terrorist group looking to buy a large business in downtown Chicago. His name is Jahir Mizra. We believe he assists his family in the sale of military-grade weapons to Hamas and launders the money through their legitimate businesses. He's our link to finding out who is selling US weapons to the terrorist group. Mizra comes from one of the wealthiest families in Dubai, a family known for being Hamas sympathizers. He runs in elite social circles and enjoys traveling to our country frequently. Our intel indicates he recently set up a shell company and has been in contact with Cahill Investment Bankers. I need you to find out which shell company is his and let me know when he is close to purchasing a building. If we can prove he is laundering money through a company on American soil, we can get him. Can you do that?"

Oliver's face went pale at the thought. "If you know all of this, why haven't you already grabbed him?"

Kirkland was visibly irritated at being questioned. "Because he has a lot of influential friends, and we can't touch him until he buys a company and starts putting money into it. There's a clock ticking on this. It's rumored Hamas is planning an attack in the US. Are you sure you're up for it? We don't have time to fuck around with this."

Oliver put his head in his hands. He could feel they were wet with cold sweat.

"Oliver?" Kirkland asked more sternly.

The reality of the situation hit him like a gut-punch. His whole family was involved in this, except for Anna. He nodded to Kirkland in agreement.

"I think you could turn my mother. She's the attorney setting up these shell companies. My belief is she is doing it out of fear of my father."

"Would you like me to talk to your garbage man, too? Just be happy you have immunity. If I find out you talk to anyone— and I mean anyone—aside from your lawyer or these two special agents, the deal is off!"

Oliver flinched as Kirkland shouted in his face.

"I won't. I promise."

"Good boy. Now, how long until you can get us what we need?" Kirkland's question was more of a demand.

"I need time to locate Mizra's company. I'll request to handle his file. My father is always encouraging me to take on bigger clients. If I can take over his file, I'll keep you up to date on a weekly basis, or more frequently if necessary. If someone is already knee-deep in his file, I'll have to be careful in my updates.

"Tonight is our company Christmas party at The Peninsula. Our biggest clients will be there. Do you have a picture of Mizra? If he's there, I can at least make contact and develop a rapport."

Kate extracted a single picture from her leather binder. It was a zoom shot of him at a party. The definition was excellent.

"Jahir 'Jay' Mizra is thirty-two years old and five foot ten inches tall. As you can see, his hair is black with a well-groomed fade, goatee and blue eyes. He's well dressed and charismatic—"

29

Kirkland interrupted. "If he is there, don't approach him unless you think you can do so calmly."

"I can do that." Oliver sounded more confident than he felt.

"I expect you to live up to this immunity agreement."

With that, Kirkland stood, put all the evidence back in the shopping bag, grabbed it and his briefcase and left. Oxygen seemed to fill the room again, and the remaining occupants breathed easier.

"Listen," Mike sighed. "Kirkland is a pompous ass. Don't let him get to you. Text us if you need anything, and we will arrange to meet on Monday."

Oliver stood and shook both the special agents' hands. Mike had lifted about ten pounds of the hundred-pound weight he felt on his shoulders.

By the time Oliver got back in his car to make the forty-minute drive back home, he felt physically and emotionally drained. He turned up his radio to block out the thoughts in his head and put his brain on autopilot until he reached the parking garage for his building. He couldn't get upstairs and pour a Scotch fast enough. Dread filled him at the thought of dressing for the party, but he could hardly make an excuse not to show. Not now.

CHAPTER 6

December 17, 2016

Anna asked Oliver's private driver to stop at Saks Fifth Avenue on the north end of Michigan Avenue. As she stepped out of the warm car, her lungs involuntarily contracted against the frigid air. She was no stranger to the cold, but the wind whipping through the city was relentless.

She began her journey half-heartedly. The Magnificent Mile was buzzing and the holiday decorations were spectacular, but Anna felt numb. She hadn't slept, her mind reeling from the information dump she had received last night. Oliver had had months to process the fact their parents were criminals. She'd had less than twenty-four hours.

Still, here I am, the good little soldier, always doing as I'm asked.

Once inside the crowded department store, she picked out purchases with ease. Her family was so predictable in its taste it made shopping easy. She worked her way south on the avenue and had completed her final purchase at Nordstrom's by half past two.

Christmas shopping in the city had always been one of her favorite things. Now she just felt exhausted and dreaded her next destination; she was on her way to meet her mother at The Peninsula hotel.

When she gave her name to the desk clerk, he practically jumped the counter to assist her personally with her bags. Anna was perplexed at his exuberance, but only for a moment. The elevator kept climbing; her mother had reserved the ostentatious

Peninsula Suite, which was well over three thousand square feet. The clerk no doubt was expecting a large tip, and Meredith didn't disappoint him. She handed him a hundred-dollar bill after he had placed all of Anna's belongings in the second bedroom.

"Anna!" Meredith exclaimed, giving her daughter a warm embrace. "Are you ready to get pampered this afternoon? This is the first time you've made the Christmas party!"

Anna smiled but inside she was cursing her poor fortune. Her exams had always let her dodge her father's celebration of himself in previous years.

"Go put on the robe in your closet and wash your makeup off. Nora and Emma will be here soon."

Anna walked into the spacious second bedroom while her mother continued chatting about everything except what Anna really wanted to know: *How could you do something so illegal?* She couldn't help but assume it was dirty money that paid for all this excess.

Her mother's beauty team arrived while Anna was changing. The living room looked like a professional photoshoot. There were extra lights, large makeup kits and a suitcase full of hair products and accessories. In the midst of it all, Meredith was sitting in a cushioned chair. She motioned for Anna to come sit beside her. They were separated by a table filled with champagne and a fruit tray.

Anna greeted Nora and Emma. She had met them several times before; her mother didn't go to any event without professional hair and makeup.

Champagne began flowing, and as it hit Anna's stomach, she felt a relaxing warmth spread through her body. She looked at her mom and could see how happy she was to spend this time with her daughter. Anna let her judgment fade for the time being. She wanted to enjoy this special moment with her mom.

"You just sit back and relax, honey," Nora said with a smile. "You're going to be even more beautiful when I'm done." She pulled Anna's hair back with a headband to begin her makeup. "Ouch! That is quite a scar on your forehead. I bet there's a story for that!"

Before Anna could reply, Meredith jumped in. "She had a nasty fall from the uneven bars when she was in gymnastics. It looks worse than it was at the time. She only needed five stitches." She smiled and gave a sideways glance to Anna.

Anna smiled at Nora and closed her eyes as the makeup application began. She expected no different from her mother. Meredith had been lying about the one-inch scar for years, and always encouraged Anna to keep her bangs so it wouldn't "ruin her beautiful face." It wasn't from gymnastics.

Anna felt her stomach tighten as her mind returned to the memory. She'd been eight years old when she, out of curiosity, entered Tommy's room. No one was allowed to go into his room except for her parents, by Thomas' order; it remained exactly as it was the day Tommy died. But Anna was a child, and she wanted to know more about her oldest brother. Her mother was working in her home office and her father wasn't expected for another hour. Gingerly, she turned the handle on the door and entered.

Anna was fascinated by Tommy's room. This was the first time he felt real to her. Lined up on his dresser was a Little League trophy along with a picture of Tommy and her dad. Thomas was smiling. The resemblance between father and son was unmistakable. As she sat on the floor in front of the dresser, Anna felt sorry for her dad. His love for Tommy was obvious.

Sitting there, she tried to memorize everything in the room. Her own heart hurt for the brother she never knew.

Time passed quickly, and Anna never heard Thomas come up the stairs. When he saw Tommy's door open and the little girl sitting on the floor, his temper raged. Thomas, with his shock of black hair and deep-set blue eyes, was imposing at five foot eleven inches tall. He had the build of a linebacker. To Anna, he was terrifying.

She remembered how he'd pulled her up to her feet and smacked her across the face with his beefy hand. The force of the blow knocked her into the doorframe; the skin on her forehead split as she hit the strike plate on the door jamb. She screamed in pain, but he pulled her up again and threw her into the hallway. Meredith, hearing the ruckus, came running around the corner from her office. She yelled at Thomas, who was red-faced and clenching his fists. Furious, she shoved her husband into the wall. He grabbed her wrists tightly.

"Keep your street rat out of my son's room!" Thomas pushed Meredith back, releasing her wrists. He stormed downstairs to his study and slammed the door.

Meredith quickly turned to Anna, who was bleeding profusely from her head and dazed by the attack. She knew she couldn't take her daughter to the emergency room; she could explain away the cut but not the red welt in the shape of a handprint on her face. Instead, she called her neighbor who was a nurse. She stitched up Anna's forehead with a worried glance to Meredith. The neighbor was sworn to secrecy, and Meredith promised Thomas would never touch Anna again.

In addition to the stitches, Anna had a black eye and swollen lip. She missed two weeks of school, waiting for all the evidence of abuse to dissipate. Meredith told the school she had bronchitis. No one asked any questions when Anna returned, quiet and withdrawn.

She never dared to enter Tommy's room again and kept a wide berth from her father. Meredith pretended nothing happened. Oliver could hear his sister crying herself to sleep at night. A part of him had wanted to go comfort her, but he didn't dare incur his father's wrath.

"There, all done!" Nora declared. She held a mirror up for Anna to look at her handiwork.

She wasn't used to wearing this much makeup, but Nora had outdone herself. Anna thanked her as Emma stepped in to do her hair. Again, Anna closed her eyes and let the buzz of the champagne relax her. Emma crafted her long blonde hair into an intricate twist that ended neatly at the nape of her neck. Anna marveled at the style. She could only manage a ponytail or French braid by herself.

"Thank you, Emma. I love the twist. It's beautiful!"

Meredith added her agreement. "You two are brilliant as always. I don't know what I'd do without you."

Anna could tell the champagne was hitting her mother, too. The girls packed up their gear and left happy with a large bonus from Meredith.

Anna headed into the bedroom to get dressed, but Meredith stopped her.

"Come here, sweetheart. I have something to give you for tonight."

Meredith pulled out a black velvet box from her robe pocket. Anna gasped when she saw her mother's diamond and sapphire drop earrings.

"Mom, I can't borrow these! They're too expensive. What if I lose one?"

"You won't, and they'll go perfect with your dress, along with this." Meredith reached in her other pocket and pulled out a matching three-strand bracelet.

Anna hugged her mother and felt the warmth of her love returned. Her mother, the criminal. She shoved back the thought as it crept into her conscience.

"Now go get dressed and we will meet back in the living room for a girl check," Meredith said with a big smile.

Anna dressed and looked in the full-length mirror. With her hair and makeup done and the added accessories, she truly felt beautiful.

Her mother got teary-eyed when Anna met her in the living room.

"Anna, you are stunning!"

Meredith was wearing an emerald-colored velvet gown with a bateau neckline and a side slit up to her knee. She finished her look with a diamond princess necklace and matching knot earrings.

"Mom, you are breathtaking," Anna said sincerely. "Dad will be blown away!"

Meredith laughed. "Really, Anna. We both know your father hasn't looked at me in years. Now, let's head down to the Water Tower ballroom."

Anna felt a little bit sick at her mother's comment. She and Oliver were aware of their father's chain of mistresses. He rarely stayed at the house in Winnetka, preferring the company condo in Chicago. Anna knew her mother was no fool, but to hear her refer to her father's affairs so flippantly was unsettling. It also renewed Anna's disgust toward her father. Despite her mother's comment, Anna knew the affairs hurt her deeply.

She told Meredith she needed a few more minutes and would meet her downstairs. Meredith gave her a wink and headed out of the suite. Anna breathed a sigh of relief. She needed to prepare herself for seeing her father. She hadn't seen him since August when she left for school. She wasn't even sure if he knew she would be in attendance tonight.

Anna threw back one more glass of champagne and took a deep breath before heading downstairs.

As she entered the ballroom, three sets of eyes locked onto her—for three different reasons.

CHAPTER 7

March 10, 2017

Mike Mallory climbed into his FBI-issue black sedan and called his supervisor. It was six o'clock in the evening, but he knew his boss would be waiting to give him an earful.

Supervisory Special Agent Jack Harland answered on the second ring. "Mallory, I've been trying to get a hold of you. What the hell is going on with the Cahill investigation? Four homicides, our CI is critically wounded and you left the scene?"

"Sir, I can explain everything. We have a delicate situation, and I have something I need you to see. Are you still at the office?"

"Where else would I be on a Friday night?" Harland answered sarcastically.

"I'll be there in fifteen."

"This better be good, or you and DeSoto are off the case."

Mike heard the dial tone and swore under his breath. He and Kate had taken a big risk removing Anna Cahill from the murder scene, sight unseen. He gripped the steering wheel and prayed Harland would understand when he saw her video statement.

He pulled out of the hotel parking garage and made his way toward Roosevelt Road, where the FBI field office was located. The vein in his forehead bulged as he hit heavy traffic.

"Of course it would be fucking rush hour in downtown Chicago!"

He hit his lights and siren and sped in and out of traffic until he reached headquarters.

Harland was on the phone when Mike walked into his office. He motioned for him to take a seat. Mike listened to his supervisor speak with the Cook County sheriff.

"I understand you have pressure from the press. This is a quadruple homicide with three of the deceased individuals under federal investigation. Please leave out the identities of the victims and the lone survivor until tomorrow night. We need to evaluate the situation. If the details get out now, we'll lose months of work. I understand. Again, we appreciate your cooperation."

He replaced the receiver and glared at Mike. "We're three days from shutting down Cahill Investment Bankers and the whole family is dead except for our informant. Tell me what the hell is going on!"

Mike flinched at his tone. Harland was normally a quiet man, but Mike knew he had been getting a lot of heat from the chief federal prosecutor to make this case.

"Sir." Mike took out his phone, queued up the video and handed it to Harland. "When we arrived at the scene, we found Anna Cahill hiding in her closet. She witnessed the event. No one knows she's in town. Based on the assassinations today, I believe our operation is compromised. Special Agent DeSoto and I removed her from the scene without anyone knowing she was present. DeSoto is with her at a hotel right now. You're familiar with the clientele at the Cahill firm; her life could be in danger if they think she knows something. Please, watch her statement."

Mike sat quietly while Harland played the video. Once it finished, Harland sat silently for a minute, his hand rubbing his face in frustration and disbelief.

"No one saw her?"

"No, sir. She called my personal cell right after the shootings. She hid in her closet until we came and got her. DeSoto and I were able to take her down the back stairs and get her in our car without anyone seeing."

"How did she come to have your personal cell?"

"Oliver was concerned because she went on a date with Mizra. They met at the company Christmas party. He urged her to stay away from Mizra but couldn't give her the real reason why. Instead, he gave her my card and told her they had a disgruntled client and to call me if the guy ever bothered her."

Harland nodded for Mike to continue.

"Oliver is currently in critical condition, having undergone surgery to repair his femoral artery. I'm sure the police have a presence at Evanston Hospital, but I think we need to have agents there as well. Certain people may not want him to wake up."

Harland picked up the phone and dispatched two field agents to babysit Oliver. They would notify him once he was conscious.

"I understand your actions, Mallory," he said, "but you should have called me immediately when you found the girl. You may be a seasoned agent, but you are not in charge of this investigation. That being said, let's get her to a safe house tonight."

"Does anyone have eyes on Mizra?" Mike asked, concerned he would try to flee once news of the murders came out.

"We picked him up today on his way to the airport. He was booked on a flight home to Dubai. A little convenient if you ask me."

"Has anyone questioned him yet?"

"Kirkland is coming in tomorrow afternoon. He doesn't want anyone to talk to Mizra until he is present to watch the interview." Harland looked at Mike with exasperation.

"Can't wait," Mike said sarcastically.

Harland handed him a piece of paper with an address on it. The house was in Naperville, a safe distance from Winnetka and the city.

"You and DeSoto take her, and I'll have additional field agents meet you there. We need to keep her hidden until we find out if her brother is going to survive the night and what, if anything, she is hiding from us."

Mike stood to leave. Harland said, as much to himself as to him, "My gut says Mizra is our guy. He may not have pulled the trigger, but I bet he ordered the hit. Still, we can't narrow the field to just him. Every blacklisted client is going to be trying to cover his tracks by any means necessary."

On his way back to the hotel, Mike called Kate to tell her to get Anna ready for the trip to the safe house. He would be there soon.

CHAPTER 8

March 11, 2017

Anna sat upright on the bed in a panic. It took a few minutes for her to recognize her new surroundings. She had been in a daze when they reached the safe house. She had no idea how long she had been out—she didn't even remember falling asleep—but it was still dark outside.

She exited the bedroom she was in and peered down the hallway. There appeared to be three more bedrooms. She headed for the stairwell and the voices she heard coming from downstairs. There was a beautifully decorated great room, complete with sectional sofa, flat-screen TV and fireplace. Beyond that, she could see the kitchen, which was partially open to the great room. She was in an upscale home. She'd always imagined safe houses as rundown structures in bad neighborhoods with bars on the windows.

Anna stood in the kitchen doorway for a moment, watching the new agents, busy on their laptops, before they spied her.

"Were you able to sleep?" asked the young blond agent, who couldn't have been more than thirty. He stood and introduced himself. "I'm SA Garrett. This is SA McCormack."

McCormack was in his early fifties, built like a bulldog with a gray crewcut.

"How long was I out for? What time is it?" Anna asked. She needed to get to Oliver.

"Here, take a seat." Garrett pulled a chair out for her and Anna obeyed. "You were down for a few hours. It's two o'clock in the morning. Agents DeSoto and Mallory will be back around eight o'clock. Do you want something to drink or eat?"

"Can I have a Coke, please? I have a terrible migraine. Do you have any acetaminophen?"

"Sure. The house is well stocked. You can help yourself to whatever you want at any time." SA Garrett fetched Anna the drink and medicine for her head.

"You should really try to eat something," McCormack said. "When was the last time you put something in your stomach?"

Anna sat and thought for a moment. The past twelve hours felt like days. "I don't remember."

Garrett put a donut on a plate and placed it in front of her. "If that doesn't appeal to you, I'll be happy to make you something."

"It's fine, thank you." Anna took the medicine and a bite of the donut. "Can I see Oliver? How is he?" The full enormity of the previous day's events was beginning to sink in.

McCormack chimed in. "He's in ICU. The surgery to repair his femoral artery went well. The doctors are waiting for him to regain consciousness. Don't worry, we have agents at the hospital guarding him."

Anna forced herself to eat the donut, anything to ease the throbbing in her head. "What are you both looking at?" she asked as she took a long sip of her Coke.

Garrett exchanged a glance with McCormack, who nodded slightly. "We are going through surveillance footage, trying to identify the shooter. He didn't have ID on him. Do you remember any more details about him, outside of him being a bald man with a scar on the back of his head?"

Anna put her hand over her eyes, both in pain and in thought. A few minutes passed and the agents quietly went back to reviewing footage.

"Oh my God!" Anna whispered. Both agents looked up at her. "Jay's driver. He has a scar on the back of his head. I've been in the back seat of his car and stared at it. But Jay couldn't be involved in this."

"Jay?" SA Garrett asked, confused.

"Jahir. Jahir Mizra. He goes by Jay, or at least that's what he told me to call him."

"You know Jahir Mizra?" McCormack asked incredulously.

"He's one of my brother's clients. We've been dating since December. I met him at the company Christmas party."

"Do Mallory and DeSoto know about this?" Garrett asked, dumbstruck.

"I'm not sure. Oliver knew and he wasn't happy about it. He's my big brother. He'd be critical of anyone I dated."

"Wait." Garrett made some notes on his pad of paper. "Are you still in contact with Mizra?"

"We usually text every day. I haven't been able to talk to him much lately because I've had midterms. He knows it's important for me to focus on graduating in May."

"Did he know you were coming home yesterday?" McCormack asked, trying to keep his voice even.

"No. I was going to surprise him after I saw my parents. He was hoping I would get into Northwestern Pritzker School of Law so I would be back in Chicago. I wanted to tell my parents first."

Garrett looked at her in disbelief.

McCormack picked up a manila folder with photographs inside. "Anna, would you look at these pictures and identify anyone you recognize?"

Anna opened the folder and held up the top picture. "This is Jay…" Confusion settled in her brain. "Why do you have his picture?"

Garrett pointed back to the folder. "Please, Anna, just keep going."

She flipped to the next few pictures. She recognized the faces but wasn't sure exactly who they were. "I think these men might have provided him with security. I don't know their names and they weren't around on our dates; at least, not that I noticed." Anna picked up the final photo. "This is him. This is Jay's driver, but I don't know his name either."

Garrett and McCormack watched Anna's face as the puzzle pieces started coming together. She shook her head slowly as she looked through the pictures a second time.

Her eyes snapped to Garrett, who was sitting across from her. "This can't be. It would mean Jay is behind the murders. Why would he do that?" Realization was spreading through her body, quickly dispelling the cloud she had been in for almost four months.

Anna ran to the kitchen trash bin and swiftly released the donut she had just eaten. Could Jay really have given the order for the assassinations? She sat on the floor of the kitchen and cried.

Garrett helped her up and led her to the sofa in the next room. He handed her a box of tissues and sat quietly next to her until her sobs subsided and disbelief returned.

"Maybe it was his dad. Jay told me his dad is an exceedingly difficult man. I think he's afraid of him. That's why he came to the US, to build his own commercial real estate business and get out from under his father." Anna looked hopefully at Garrett. Her heart was aching, and she needed to hear it wasn't Jay who was responsible.

"We're still investigating. Let's not jump to any conclusions."

Anna wiped her tears and nodded.

***

McCormack stepped into the office off the kitchen and closed the door. He phoned Mike. He hated to wake him, but he needed to be apprised of the current situation.

He answered on the third ring. "This is Mallory," he said quietly as he slipped out of bed and closed the door. His wife was used to late night calls, but he hated to wake her.

"Mike, this is Will McCormack. I'm sorry to disturb you, but we got a positive ID on the shooter from Anna Cahill. It's Jahir Mizra's driver, but we don't have a name. I was hoping you might have it in your notes so we can update Harland."

"How did you get that out of her? We talked to her for hours and she didn't remember." Mike was now wide awake and a little annoyed that precious time had been wasted.

McCormack filled Mike in on the sequence of events that lead to her identification. Papers rustled on the other end of the phone.

"His name is Aalam Barakat. He goes by 'Al,'" Mike said eventually. "Mizra was picked up yesterday heading for the airport. Barakat had a residence in the city. I'll work on getting a warrant to search his place for anything tying this hit to someone."

"One more thing." McCormack wasn't ready to let it go. "Were you aware Anna Cahill was dating Jahir Mizra? That they were in contact by text until a couple of days ago?"

"They went on a few dates over her winter break. I didn't think it went any further than that. She had no idea we were investigating him."

"Well, she's figured it out now. She said it could be his father. Jahir intimated he was trying to get away from his father by coming to the US. I don't know if her theory holds water or if it's just a coping mechanism—she just realized the guy she's dating likely hired an assassin to kill her family."

"Let me get dressed and I'll be there within the hour. Try to keep her calm. She has a prescription for anxiety if she has a panic attack. Kate and I witnessed one when we took her initial statement. It's rough."

Mike hung up the phone and cursed silently. He called Harland and got approval to enter the driver's residence. Harland would take care of the paperwork. Mike then called another agent he trusted and told him to take a team to Barakat's address.

At least they had the identity of their shooter for Kirkland tomorrow.

CHAPTER 9

December 17, 2016

Anna's face lit up when she walked into the Water Tower ballroom. As usual, her mother had made sure the decorations were festive and elegant. The perimeter of the room was draped in tiny white lights, giving it a romantic glow. There were Christmas trees in all four corners, each decorated in a different theme. At each place setting, a silver-dipped pinecone ornament was placed as a keepsake.

"Anna!" Oliver called a little too loudly.

Startled, she looked toward her brother's voice. He was standing with her father and a handsome gentleman she had never seen before. She smiled and walked over to the group. The champagne was making her giddy. She sidled up to her father and gave him a kiss on his cheek, stifling a giggle as he stiffened at the contact.

"Hi, Dad. I finally made it to one of your parties." Anna winked at him. She moved on to her brother and gave him a kiss on his cheek.

"Anna, you look..." Oliver searched for the right word.

"Exquisite." The attractive stranger completed Oliver's sentence.

Anna blushed. He reached for her hand and she felt a spark.

"I'm Jahir Mizra, but please call me Jay."

"Hello, Jay. I'm Anna Cahill." She gently pulled her hand back to her, without breaking eye contact.

"Jay is a new client of ours. He's from Dubai and looking to purchase a few hotels in Chicago." Oliver kept his voice cheerful, although he didn't like the chemistry between his sister and a top FBI suspect.

"Thomas, you didn't tell me you had a daughter," chided Jay.

Thomas tried to smile but it looked more like a grimace. "Anna is our adopted daughter." He let out an awkward chuckle. The other three looked at him sideways. He quickly realized his statement was inappropriate and tried to sound fatherly. "She's just finishing up at Ohio State University."

"Really? What are you studying?" Jay asked.

"My major is political science with a minor in psychology."

"She's made the dean's list every semester," Oliver bragged, not for Jay's benefit but for his father's. He was irritated that Thomas always made Anna feel like an outcast. "Anna, I think Mom's looking for you," he added, trying to get her away from Jay.

"Of course," Anna said. "Perhaps later you can tell me about Dubai," she told Jay, then nodded to them all as she went off in search of her mother.

Meredith had already spotted her daughter, and met her halfway across the ballroom. "I see you've met the company's newest client. He can't seem to take his eyes off you."

"Mom, really," Anna demurred. She took her mother by the arm and walked over to a table of hors d'oeuvres. "I'm starving!"

Anna piled some of the more appealing items onto a plate and grabbed a glass of Riesling from the bartender. Meredith was right in step.

"Do you know he comes from a very wealthy family in Dubai? Not to mention his own net worth is twenty million dollars," she cooed.

"Mom, are you seriously trying to pimp me out to a rich client?" Anna laughed.

"Oh, stop. I'm just trying to point you toward quality men. You're too mature for college boys, which is probably why you haven't had a boyfriend in two years."

"I get the impression Dad doesn't want me here, least of all monopolizing such a big client." She'd expected as much, but still felt a twinge of disappointment.

"Forget your father. He brought his young new 'assistant' to keep him company tonight." Bitterness seeped into Meredith's tone.

Anna watched her take the last sip of her Old Fashioned and signal the bartender for another. Once she had her next drink in hand, she led Anna over to the tables.

Anna couldn't help but ask the obvious question.

"Mom," she whispered, "why don't you just divorce Dad?"

Meredith looked at her daughter with amusement. "Now, why would I do that?" She smoothly moved some place cards around so that Jahir Mizra would be sitting next to Anna and at a different table than Thomas. "There, now you won't be bored tonight, and judging from the fact he keeps looking at you, neither will he!"

Meredith knew Thomas would be furious. She moved back to the head table and took the assistant's place card from beside Thomas' and switched it with someone at a back table. She smiled wickedly.

Anna would have to keep an eye on her mother tonight. She only drank occasionally, but she had already switched from champagne to a very strong cocktail.

A small bell rang as the ballroom doors were closed over, signaling everyone to find their designated seats for the plated dinner. Anna had mentioned her preference for a buffet, but it wouldn't be "upscale" enough according to her mother. At least the guests had a choice between beef, seafood or chicken.

As Anna made her way to her table, she spotted Jay standing next to her chair. He pulled it out for her as she approached and waited until she was settled to take his own seat. Anna gave him a shy smile.

"This must be kismet, us seated beside each other," Jay said, smiling.

Anna laughed. "More like a meddling mother."

"Well, remind me to thank her. I was dreading this party until you walked in the room." Jay looked at her sincerely.

Blushing, Anna changed the subject. "I'm curious, why does a man from Dubai have a British accent?"

"I love how Americans get right to the point," he said with a smile. "I was born in Qatar, but my parents moved to Dubai when I was two years old. At the age of ten, I was sent to boarding school in England. From there, I went to Oxford for four years to obtain my master's degree in business. So, I guess twelve years as a British resident rubbed off on me."

"But now you live in Dubai?" Anna kept the disappointment out of her voice.

"Yes, but I am moving my business operations to the US. That's why I want to purchase a couple of hotels here in Chicago. I'm hoping to make this my permanent residence."

"Do you have any family still in Dubai?" Anna worried she was peppering him with too many questions, but she couldn't help herself and he didn't seem to mind answering.

"My parents are in Dubai. My father has a successful commercial real estate business there. I have one sister, who is several years older than me. I was still a boy when she got married. Her husband joined my father in business. After a twelve-year absence, I was a bit of the odd man out at my father's company. That's why he is supportive of me expanding my horizons and building my own enterprise in the United States.

"Now, my turn. You seem close to your mother and Oliver, but I noticed a chill with you and your father. What is that about? Are you a wild child?" he asked jokingly.

Anna gave him an abbreviated version of how she came to be adopted, and admitted her father had been against it and still ignored her as much as possible. She could tell Jay was disturbed by her father's behavior.

"Please don't let that influence your decision to work with Cahill Investment." Anna was aware there was a pleading tone to her voice. "Oliver is incredible at his job and will take care of you."

Jay gave her a big smile. "I wouldn't dream of leaving, especially now that I've met you."

Anna relaxed.

"Besides, I know what it's like to have a father who is tough on you. My father treated me like a stranger when I returned from university. It's a bit ironic, since he's the one who sent me to another country in the first place. I thought I was being groomed to take over his business, but my brother-in-law insinuated himself into my dad's grand plan while I was away. I'm not very close with my sister or her family."

"I'm so sorry," Anna replied. "That must be very difficult for you."

Jay shrugged. "I think it's better to have this freedom. I'm much more influenced by Western culture while my family is very strict Sunni Muslim. See…" He held up his wine glass. "They wouldn't be happy about this."

Anna and Jay talked non-stop through dinner. She felt butterflies in her stomach, which had never happened before. His interest was piqued as well. They exchanged numbers so they could arrange a dinner the following week.

"This is my private number. I only give it out to beautiful girls named Anna," Jay flirted as Anna jokingly rolled her eyes.

"Seriously, do you have two different phones?"

"I do but it's not for anything suspicious. My family and my business associates have the number of my main phone. I prefer to keep a separate phone for people who are close to me. It never gets turned off, so if a friend needs me, I am always available. I'm hoping you will give me a chance to get to know you."

Anna smiled and blushed.

"Please, though, don't mention it to your brother. I don't want him to be offended."

Anna assured him it was their secret.

As dessert was being served, Thomas moved to the front of the ballroom with a microphone to give his annual speech. Anna texted Jay that her father could be long-winded. The two spent the entire speech texting under the table and trying to contain their laughter.

Oliver had been staring at them from a nearby table throughout the dinner. He was in a panic over what to do. He went to the nearest restroom and texted SA Mallory, asking him how to proceed. Mike responded Oliver shouldn't be concerned at this early stage, and that he should use any opportunity available to develop a closer relationship with Jahir. The FBI would intercede if it became necessary.

CHAPTER 10

March 11, 2017

Oliver's head felt thick, like a hard-drinking hangover. A steady beeping added to his discomfort. He opened his eyes and noticed an IV inserted into his right hand and several leads coming out of his hospital gown. As he fought to focus, he felt a throbbing pain in his right leg. Panic gripped him, and his breaths came fast.

The beeping quickened and a nurse quickly appeared by his side.

"Oliver, take a deep breath. You're ok. Hold on, let me get you some water. You've been unconscious for quite a while." She continued speaking to him in a soothing voice as she poured him a glass from a pitcher on the bedside table. "I'm Stella; I'll be your nurse today. I can get you something for the pain if you need."

Oliver gulped down the water and nodded to her. Another face came into view. It was Mike. A feeling of dread fell on his chest like a fifty-pound weight as his memory of the previous day came flooding back.

"Not too long," Stella said sternly to Mike. "He had a rough night and needs to rest." She turned to Oliver. "I'll be right back with something for the pain."

Mike interjected, "Can you hold off on giving him anything for fifteen minutes? I need him to be lucid while I ask him a few questions."

Stella pursed her lips and looked at Oliver.

"I can wait," he said.

"Alright." She looked back at Mike. "Fifteen minutes, no more. I'll bring you a mild sedative, as well, so you can sleep," she told

Oliver, then gave a last firm look at Mike as a silent warning not to agitate her patient.

As she exited the room, Oliver noticed two FBI agents posted outside his door. Somehow it didn't comfort him.

"Where is my family?" he asked with trepidation.

Mike didn't need to say a word. Oliver could see by the agent's expression that they were gone. He put his hands over his eyes and wept.

"I need to call Anna," he realized. "She could be in danger!"

"We have her. She's in a safe house." Mike pulled a chair up to Oliver's bedside. "Listen, I know this is difficult, but I need you to tell me exactly what happened yesterday."

Oliver wiped his eyes on his sheet and handed his cup to Mike for more water. He drank it while Mike took out his phone and hit the record button.

"Start from the beginning. How did you all wind up at your parents' house in Winnetka?"

Oliver took a ragged breath. "My mom sent me a text message around twelve-thirty that I needed to come home. I tried calling her, but she didn't answer. I left the office and drove as fast as I could. When I got to the house, it was a little after one o'clock. I saw my dad and David pulling up. They'd gotten the same message. We walked in and another man was standing in the doorway of the study. My mom was sitting in a chair, crying."

Oliver paused for a moment. Tears were flowing down his face. Mike hated to be pushy, but he had to get a statement from him. Kirkland was en route from DC and he wanted answers.

"Oliver, I need to know what happened."

Oliver took a deep breath. "He motioned for us to come into the study. He had a gun in his waistband and kept his hand on it. My dad demanded to know what was going on."

"Did you recognize this man? There was no sign of forced entry."

"Yeah, he was Mizra's driver. I'd seen him a couple of times when I met Jay at some properties. His name is Al. He started ranting. He knew Jay was under investigation and wanted to know the identity of the snitch. No one knew what he was talking about, except for me. My dad is a big man and has a bad temper. He yelled at Al that he was crazy and to get the fuck out of his house."

Oliver hesitated.

"I'm sorry to push you," Mike said, "but we need to know exactly what happened."

"When my dad stepped toward him, Al shot him. Then he shot David and my mom in quick succession. I jumped on him to get the gun away."

At this point, his recollection aligned with Anna's. Mike let Oliver finish with the recording running so he would be able to provide Kirkland with corroboration of events.

Oliver's tears turned to anger. "I did everything you asked. You messed up and got my family killed! Do you think I feel safe with your agents at my door? For all I know, one of them might try to kill me."

Oliver's voice was rising, and Mike was worried it would carry through the closed door.

He leaned in closer. "Listen, Al was dead when the EMTs arrived at your house. We realize someone in the Bureau leaked information. Agents are searching Al's home. We are trying to find out who ordered this. These agents"—he motioned to the door—"check out. I wouldn't put you in further danger."

The door opened and Stella entered with two syringes. Oliver was glad to see her. His pain was intense and his head felt ready to explode. If Anna was safe for now, he could rest.

He had one more question as his medicine was administered. "When can I see my sister?"

"It may be a while before that happens. We need to keep you both out of harm's way."

"Tell her I love her and I'm ok. I…" Oliver tried to continue but the pain medicine and sedative cocktail kicked in.

Stella looked at Mike, who promptly left. He had gotten all the information he needed.

CHAPTER 11

December 19, 2016

Anna strode into the bank at nine o'clock sharp, Monday morning. She sat patiently waiting for the bank manager to call her into his office. With an account of just over one million dollars and the last name Cahill, she received top-shelf treatment.

"Anna Cahill?"

She turned to see a short man with receding, dyed black hair and glasses. She smiled and stood up.

He shook her hand firmly. "I'm Robert Milton. I understand you would like to discuss your savings account with us?" Anna nodded and he ushered her into his office. "How can I be of assistance?"

Anna placed the letter from the attorney on his desk. "I have an UTMA account that came to maturation last year. I was never notified, and I would like to have my father's name removed from the account."

Milton typed in the account number on his computer and moved the screen so she could see it as well. "Here we are. It shows Thomas Cahill as custodian. He is your father, correct?"

"Yes. As you can see, his custodianship ended when I turned twenty-one. I am now twenty-two and would like him removed from the account."

"So, you would like to keep your account with us?" Robert asked hopefully. Anna nodded. "Wonderful. I just need to see your driver's license to confirm your age and one other form of identification."

Anna fished her wallet out of her purse and handed him her license and Ohio State student ID. "Would you please change the mailing address to this one in Ohio?" She passed him a slip of paper with her college address.

"Not a problem. Just give me a few minutes here." He turned the screen back to face him and clacked loudly on the keys for about five minutes.

Anna's anxiety was rising as she waited. She pushed it down and asserted herself. "I'd also like my father to be barred any access to my account."

Robert Milton looked up over his glasses at Anna. She stared back at him.

He made some more changes and hit the enter key. The screen was turned back to Anna.

"No problem. As you can see, I have opened a new account in your name only and transferred all monies into it. You are the sole owner of the account and no one else will be able to access it. Currently, your account is earning about three percent on average. Would you like to discuss placing some of your money into mutual funds for a better return?"

"Thank you, but no," Anna said firmly. "If you could print me out a statement of my new account and balance, I'll be on my way."

The printer whirred on the credenza behind Milton's desk and soon she had all the information she needed in hand. She stood and he offered to walk her out. She declined and thanked him again for his assistance.

Anna walked out to the car and sat for a moment in the parking lot. She looked at the papers she was holding. Tomorrow, she would contact the bank in the Cayman Islands that Oliver had recommended and initiate a transfer of funds. A shiver ran through her as she imagined how her father would react when he found out she had taken control of the account. She would never tell him where she sent the money.

***

Anna walked into the kitchen and was greeted by her mother. Meredith was working from home all week.

"There you are! I saw the Mercedes was gone and wondered where you were off to."

"I had a few errands to run. Honestly, Mom, you can sell the car once I go back to school. I'll be done in four months, and besides, I like my car in Columbus more than the Mercedes."

"I wanted to talk to you about your plans after graduation," Meredith began.

Anna felt her stomach drop. She didn't want to reveal to her mother that she had applied to law schools until she knew she had been accepted somewhere.

"Do you intend to come back to the Chicago area?"

Anna smiled and nodded.

Meredith continued, "I'm planning on putting the house up for sale in the spring. Your father is never here, Oliver has his own place in the city and I'm sure you won't want to be living in sleepy Winnetka once you graduate. This house is too big for me to rattle around in myself."

Anna could see her mother carefully watching for her reaction. She was relieved, glad Meredith hadn't asked about her grand plan for after she received her diploma. "I think that's a great idea, Mom. I hate the idea of you being here all alone. Are you going to get a place in Chicago?"

"I haven't decided yet if I want to be downtown or get a townhome in a closer suburb. You know I will always have room for you if you need it. I don't want you to feel like I'm selling the house and leaving you homeless," Meredith stressed.

"I appreciate that, Mom," Anna said sincerely. Although she had grown up in this house, she felt no sense of loss at the thought of its sale. Her childhood memories were too mixed for that.

Worried Meredith might still ask about her future plans, Anna quickly changed the subject. "I'm going to stay at Oliver's Wednesday night," she said with a grin. She knew her mother would be ecstatic when she knew why.

"Again? You just spent Friday night there." Meredith's disappointment was evident.

"Well, I have a date and it would be easier for him to pick me up at Oliver's than drive all the way out here."

Her jaw dropped. "What! You're just telling me now? Is it with Jay Mizra, by any chance?" She looked at her like a child waiting to open a present.

"Yes!" Anna laughed. "I could really use your help picking an outfit to wear."

Meredith clapped her hands with joy. "I knew it! I knew he was interested in you! Where is he taking you?"

"The Signature Room on the 95th."

"Perfect! Well, let's go upstairs." Meredith jogged up the back staircase with Anna right behind her. "If we don't find the right thing, we can always go shopping!"

Anna was touched by her mother's enthusiasm. She wished Oliver could be as accepting of her choice of suitor.

CHAPTER 12

March 11, 2017

Mike Mallory and Kate DeSoto sat at a metal table in an otherwise bare room. The door opened, and a handcuffed Jahir Mizra entered, led by two agents. Mike was acutely aware that Chief Federal Prosecutor Kirkland was behind the glass, watching and listening. He could almost feel the prosecutor's breath on the back of his neck.

Mike hit the record button and looked directly at Mizra. "Good afternoon, Mr. Mizra. May I call you Jay?"

"Why not?" Jay was clearly irritated.

"Ok, let's start with something simple. Why were you flying back to Dubai yesterday?"

"It's where I live." He looked at Mike like he was an idiot.

Mike leaned across the table. "Let me be more specific. You came to Chicago to purchase commercial real estate. My information tells me you've made an offer on a hotel but the deal hasn't closed yet. Why leave for Dubai at this critical point in your purchase?"

"I have thirty days until I close on the property. I've already leased a condo in Chicago. I needed to go back to Dubai to arrange for the move and see my family. Your agents could have just asked me instead of throwing me in a car and holding me in a cell with no grounds."

"We do have grounds," Kate interjected. "Are you aware that members of the Cahill family were murdered yesterday at the family home in Winnetka?"

Jay appeared shocked. "What? Why?"

"That's what we would like to know. Your driver, Aalam Barakat, was identified as the shooter."

"Then why aren't you questioning him?"

"Because Mr. Barakat died at the scene of the crime. Would you know anything about that?"

"Of course not! Why would I want to harm the Cahill family? Oliver is helping me purchase my hotel, along with additional properties. Not to mention, I'm dating Anna Cahill. I would never do anything to hurt her!" Jay was flush with anger.

Mike leaned in closer to Mizra. "Can you see where we might find it suspicious that a man with direct ties to you murders three individuals and is found dead at the scene? Our theory is you ordered the assassinations and then tried to flee. Barakat getting shot at the scene of the crime was just the icing on the cake. Your trip to Dubai was to establish an alibi and protect you from extradition back to the US."

"Your theory is a load of shite! I have no motive to kill anyone in that family. I have the right to consular notification and legal representation. I'm done talking until I speak to someone from my embassy."

"Of course." Kate looked at the agents. "Please return Mr. Mizra to his holding cell until his consular representative arrives."

As Mizra stood up, he turned to Kate. "I didn't do this. Please make sure Anna is ok. I'm worried about her."

Mike turned off the recorder as Mizra was escorted out of the room. A loud knock on the glass behind them caused Mike to swear quietly under his breath. He and Kate went next door to the viewing room where Harland and Kirkland were waiting.

"What the hell was that?" Kirkland demanded.

"I don't follow." Mike was confused.

"Why did you let him off so quickly? You should have told him his representative was on the way but if he is innocent, he should keep answering your questions."

Harland jumped in. "We've got to do everything by the book. Once he asks for his consular representative, the interview must be halted."

"Not when there is a threat of terrorism!" Kirkland bellowed.

"There is no proof linking him to any terrorist activity, and the Vienna Convention is clear on a foreign national's rights," Harland firmly reminded the prosecutor.

"Now we'll never get anything out of him! This whole investigation is a bust. I'm the one who has to go back to Washington and tell them we are no closer to finding the traitor than we were months ago."

Harland kept his voice calm. "Let's not do anything yet. He may agree to another interview once he meets with someone from his embassy. My gut tells me he was truly shocked to hear of the murders."

Before Kirkland could spout off again, Mike offered Anna's theory that it could be the senior Mizra who set up the murders without Jay's knowledge.

Kirkland scowled. "I'll be at the hotel. Call me when you're going to conduct the next interview." He stormed out of the room, leaving the three agents to decide their next move.

"What if we brought Anna in and had her talk to Mizra? If he does care about her, he may be more forthcoming," Kate suggested.

"It's an idea." Harland thought about it. "Call the UAE embassy in New York. Let's see how it plays out once his representation shows up."

CHAPTER 13

December 21, 2016

Anna arrived at Oliver's building just before four o'clock. Oliver had decided to work from home so he could monitor his sister's contact with Jay.

"Do you think you packed enough?" Oliver asked sarcastically, seeing his sister's suitcase and hanging bag.

"It takes a lot to look this good!" Anna laughed. She knew Oliver wasn't pleased with her dinner plans, but she wasn't going to let him spoil her mood. She dropped her purse on the kitchen counter and placed her belongings in the guest room.

"Hey, your phone is beeping," Oliver yelled to her from the sofa, where he was staring blankly at his laptop.

Anna practically skipped over to retrieve her phone. Oliver watched as she smiled and quickly texted a response. She placed the phone on the counter and headed back into the bedroom.

"I'm going to jump in the shower. Jay is picking me up at seven o'clock. Would you let me know if my phone beeps again?"

"Whatever," Oliver said. He understood his instructions from Mike, but he couldn't stand the thought of his sister going on a date with a possible terrorist.

Anna emerged from the bedroom at a quarter to seven, transformed. The girl who'd entered his apartment in a ponytail and sweats now stood before him looking like a model, and he didn't like it one bit.

"What do you think?" Anna asked nervously. She was wearing a black sweaterdress with a square neckline. It ended a few inches above her knees and hugged her body, complementing all the right places. She'd finished off the look with calf-high black boots and a silver and onyx necklace.

Oliver sucked in his breath. "The dress is a little short, don't you think?"

"Mom is the one who picked it out. She thought it looked great," Anna spat back at him.

"You look beautiful, Anna. I'm your older brother and I don't like you going out with Jay. I'd rather you not look like you stepped off a runway."

Anna smiled at the compliment. "Jay is a great guy. I would think you would know that, since he's your client."

"Why don't you search for him on the internet? You'll see he has a tendency to date beautiful women and then leave them brokenhearted."

"It's just dinner, Oliver. Can you give me a spare key, so I don't wake you when I come in? Unless you plan on waiting up for me."

Oliver went to the kitchen and pulled an extra key out of a drawer.

"Thank you." Anna went back into the bedroom to put the key in her dress purse and give her hot-roller curls one more coat of hairspray. It was rare for her to wear her hair down, letting it fall to the bottom of her shoulder blades.

When she returned to the family room, Oliver had poured himself a Macallan.

"May I have one too? My nerves are a little fried right now." Anna smiled.

He handed her a glass with a smaller amount than his contained. The last thing he wanted was for his sister to be drunk and with Mizra. He had given Mike and Kate the location of the date, but he wasn't sure if they would be surveilling.

Anna's phone beeped and she felt butterflies. "He's downstairs. Thanks again, Oliver, for letting me crash here. I won't be too late."

She grabbed her coat, slid her phone into her purse and headed for the door.

"Be careful!" he yelled after her, but she was already on her way to the elevators.

***

Anna stepped into the lobby and found Jay waiting for her. The look on his face made her heart skip a beat. He quickly crossed the distance between them, gave her a kiss on the cheek and helped her put her coat on. Outside, his driver was waiting to open the door of a black SUV.

Once inside, Jay took her hand in his. "You look stunning. Literally, you take my breath away."

Anna blushed and hoped he couldn't see it in the dark. "Thank you." She smiled shyly.

"I have something for you. Think of it as an early Christmas present." Jay turned on the dome light in the rear of the car and produced a gift bag from behind the seat. Anna didn't have to guess where it was from. Every girl recognized Tiffany's iconic blue.

She looked at Jay with surprise.

"Go on, open it." He seemed as excited for her to open it as she was.

Inside was a rectangular box containing a diamond tennis bracelet. Judging from the size of the diamonds, Anna calculated it must be at least four carats.

"I don't know what to say. It's the most beautiful thing anyone has ever given me."

Jay grinned like a schoolboy as he fastened the bracelet around Anna's wrist. "I have to admit, it has a hidden purpose."

Anna held her breath as unwanted doubt crept into her mind. *Was Oliver right? Does he think I'll go to bed with him because he gave me an expensive bracelet?*

He held her hand and continued, "Every time you look at your wrist, you will think of me. So, I will never be far from your thoughts."

Anna smiled shyly, mentally scolding herself for letting her brother's negativity invade her thoughts. Jay gave her hand a gentle squeeze.

The driver announced their arrival at the Hancock Building. Anna wrapped her hand around Jay's arm as he escorted her inside.

The dinner felt like a dream. They were on the top floor, overlooking the city and all the festive lights on Michigan Avenue.

"So, Anna, what are your plans after graduation?" He leaned toward her. She could smell his cologne and had to work hard to concentrate on the conversation.

"Can I trust you?" she asked. In her heart she meant more than just with her answer.

His warm smile and gentle nod quieted any concerns she had.

"My parents don't know, but I have applied to a few law schools," she confessed.

"Smart, beautiful *and* ambitious. I'm impressed. I haven't met many women from wealthy families who seek out challenging careers."

Anna laughed. "You do know you sound very misogynistic with that comment?"

It was Jay's turn to blush. "I apologize. I didn't mean it to come out that way. I'm referring to personal experience. Many women I've met want to marry a wealthy man and spend the rest of their time shopping and traveling. What I meant was that you continue to surprise me. Why haven't you told your parents?"

Anna let out a sigh and looked at her plate for a moment. She didn't want to delve too deep into her dysfunctional family on the first date. "I guess I don't want to set their expectations and then fail to be accepted to a good school."

"Somehow, I doubt that'll happen. Anyone that's made the dean's list every semester has to be at the top of her class. I hope at least one of these law schools is in Chicago, for my own selfish reasons." Jay smiled, and Anna felt a rush of excitement.

"My first choice is Northwestern, right here in the heart of the city," she told him.

"Now, I'm even more motivated to make Chicago my new home. I'll be able to see you as much as you'll allow me."

The dimple in his right cheek was very distracting.

Anna knew she had a stupid grin on her face, but she couldn't help it. "I'd like that, but what if I'm only accepted at Ohio State?"

"Then, I will be flying to Columbus frequently." He reached across the table and gently held her hand. "I'm sure you've done your research and seen that I've had a... busy dating life. I want you to know I'm past all that. I'm ready to have a real relationship. I haven't stopped thinking about you since you walked into that ballroom Saturday night. Am I scaring you yet?" he asked with a nervous laugh.

"Not at all." Anna linked her fingers through his and smiled.

"I've never met anyone who was adopted before, so please tell me if I overstep. Have you ever tried to find your birth parents?"

Anna looked at her plate and then back at Jay. "I haven't," she said, though it was something she had thought about often. "My mom told me it was a closed adoption. She doesn't even know who my mother is, or my father."

"Do you find it difficult at times? Or do you not think about it?" Jay pursued.

"It's funny you ask that. The fact my dad never wanted me is hurtful. My mom is very good to me, but she never lets me forget I'm adopted. I don't know why. I think she loves me, but she is very controlling by nature. I was only eleven when Oliver left for college, but he's still my big brother and doesn't hesitate to tell me what I should do." Anna smiled.

"I'm an expert on controlling parents, as I've told you about my father. How is your mom controlling?"

"She has an image of what she wants me to be. From the time I was very young, she had me in dance, gymnastics and cheerleading. When I quit the cheerleading squad at OSU after my sophomore year, she was very disappointed. I'm too embarrassed to ask my friends, but I don't think it's normal for a mother to keep track of your weight and measurements from the age of twelve."

"Are you serious? She doesn't still monitor you?" Jay's mouth was open in shock.

Anna grimaced. "Just my weight." She paused. "I'm sorry, that is way too much information for a first date."

"No, it's not. I want to know you. I don't want to make small talk over trivial things. Besides, it makes me feel special that you would share that with me." Jay squeezed her hand, and Anna smiled with relief.

Dinner passed too quickly, and they were soon in the high-speed elevator which would return them to the lobby. As soon as the door closed, Jay leaned over and softly kissed Anna. She didn't know if it was the kiss or the speed of the lift, but her stomach reached the ground before they did.

She struggled to keep her expectations in check. After all, this was her first date in well over a year. Her intuition, however, was shouting in her ear this wasn't an ordinary date and Jay Mizra was no ordinary man.

When they reached Oliver's building, he escorted her into the lobby and pressed the elevator button for her.

"I'm going to visit one of my mates from Oxford tomorrow. He and his family live in Miami. I'll be back Monday, the twenty-sixth. Are you free on Tuesday night?"

He's nervous!

"I can't wait," Anna replied, trying her best to give a casual smile when her heart was about to explode with excitement.

Jay cupped her face and gave her a lingering kiss. "I'll keep in touch while I'm gone."

Anna nodded and fought the urge to grab him and kiss him deeply. She looked around and noticed the security guard watching them. "Have a great trip," she said instead, and squeezed his hand.

He watched her get in the elevator. "Merry Christmas!" he called after her.

After the doors closed, Anna leaned against the wall of the elevator and closed her eyes. *Careful, Anna,* she told herself. *You are falling in love.*

CHAPTER 14

December 24–25, 2016

Anna had always loved Christmas as a child. She and her mother would spend the week before making cookies and homemade decorations for the tree. Her father would even be marginally happier. Now, her mother hired a professional team to decorate the house inside and out. Anna's homemade decorations were stuffed in a box in the attic, moldering. The house was beautiful, but to Anna it felt more like a department store display than a cozy family holiday.

One tradition that remained was going to Christmas Eve Mass as a family. Anna, Meredith and Oliver squeezed into a pew at Sacred Heart church for the first Mass of the Christmas weekend. She had made all her Sacraments here and the parish still gave her a sense of peace. The Cahill family used to be a major presence at Saturday evening Mass, but after her father distanced himself from his family, her mother had felt too embarrassed to go.

During the service, Anna did something she hadn't done in quite a while. She closed her eyes with the rest of the congregation and prayed. Perched on the kneeler, she said a fervent prayer for her mother, asking God to protect her from prosecution. She felt her mother's gentle touch on her shoulder. Anna looked up and realized everyone was already off the kneelers and seated. Meredith gave her daughter a kiss on the cheek. Anna could feel her guilty conscience trying to get out of the box she had locked it in. Suddenly, she felt a pinch between her shoulder and her neck. It was Oliver. He was staring at her hard. A nearly imperceptible shake of his head told Anna he knew what she was thinking. She stared back at him, then slouched in her pew. *How does he always know what's going through my head?*

They returned home at six-thirty, and Meredith went to the kitchen to heat the pan of lasagna and garlic bread she had picked up earlier in the day from their favorite Italian restaurant. Anna went upstairs to finish some last-minute wrapping. Per their recent family tradition, after dinner the three of them would relax in the media room, watching movies. They each got to pick one, and her mother's choice was always first—she could never last past the first movie. Oliver and Anna were the ones staying up until the wee hours of Christmas morning.

Oliver came strolling into Anna's room while she was putting the finishing touches on the last present. She looked up and noticed he was carrying a gift bag.

"Shouldn't that go under the tree?"

"This is a present for you, and I don't think you want to open it in front of Mom and Dad tomorrow."

Anna looked at him quizzically. "Ok, I'm curious. Should I open it now?"

Oliver rolled his eyes. "Yes, that is why I'm hand-delivering it to you. Open it already!"

He sat on the bed next to her as she reached into the bag and pulled out a rectangular box. "This is a DNA genealogy kit," she stated, as much to herself as to Oliver.

"I took one of these a couple of years ago," he started to explain, excitement building in him. "It tells you what your ethnicity percentages are and will send you possible matches. I've gotten a couple that are listed as third or fourth cousins. To me, the most interesting part was where my ancestors came from. Of course, Ireland and England were the biggest pieces of my ancestry wheel. Our great-grandfather emigrated from County Kerry when he was a teenager. Mom's family supposedly links back to the original colonies."

"Obviously, my ancestral makeup is going to be much different than yours. Do you think I might find my biological family doing this?" Hope and trepidation mixed uncomfortably in Anna's stomach. Now she understood why Oliver didn't want her opening it in front of her mother.

She scoffed aloud at the thought of her father even caring.

"What? You don't like it?" Oliver's disappointment was in every word.

"No, I do. I'm just a little scared to see what I might find out. After all, my birth parents gave me up for adoption, a closed adoption. They didn't want me to know who they are."

"Not true! For all you know, your mother could have been a teenager who was forced to give her baby up by her parents. All you have to do is spit in the container, mail it in and they will email you once the analysis is done. If you get a match, let me know and we can contact them together. You don't even have to contact them at all if you don't want to."

Oliver was trying hard to push down his frustration. Anna wasn't usually someone who wavered when it came to stepping into the unknown.

"You've been talking to me about finding your birth parents since you were sixteen," he kept on. "This may not give you the answers you want, but at least it's a start and you'll know where your ancestors came from."

A voice in her head was screaming at her not to do this. She was afraid of what she would find, but Oliver had gone out of his way to be thoughtful and supportive. She nodded and gave her brother a big hug. "Thank you. I'll do it."

"Good! You can do it tonight once Mom goes to bed. I'll show you how to register online. I can take the box and mail it for you."

Anna wanted to bargain for more time, but Oliver was already heading out the door, heeding Meredith's call to dinner.

***

Christmas morning was tranquil. Oliver and Anna lounged in their pajamas, bellies full, by the fireplace in front of the tree. Meredith had outdone herself with breakfast. Since she had ordered Christmas dinner in advance, she decided to make a full meal of scrambled eggs, bacon, sausage and pancakes. Anna never ceased to be surprised at the energy her mother had. After breakfast, she'd gone straight to the basement and run three miles on the treadmill before heading upstairs to get ready for the day.

Another Cahill Christmas tradition was dressing up for presents and dinner, even when it was only immediate family. At eleven o'clock, Anna and Oliver dragged themselves upstairs to get ready for their father's arrival and the end of their pleasant holiday.

Thomas would arrive by one o'clock to open the presents and have a formal dinner. Anna always felt like she was walking on eggshells when her father was home, however briefly, but this Christmas, she'd decided she wouldn't let his ill humor ruin her fun. She had been receiving texts multiple times a day from Jay and they would have marathon phone conversations late into the night. She was floating on air and refused to be knocked off her cloud.

Thomas arrived on time, carrying a bag filled with store-wrapped gifts. Anna was certain his assistant had bought them for him. As he walked into the great room, he placed the bag under the tree, removed his coat and took a seat in the leather recliner next to the fireplace. Oliver, Meredith and Anna had been sitting around the tree, drinking hot cocoa and reminiscing about Christmases long past.

"Shall we get started? I'd like to be back in the city before six o'clock." The irritation in Thomas' voice was unmistakable.

Meredith looked at her children. They both rose and began to pass out the presents. As Anna handed a gift to her father, he noticed the diamond bracelet glittering on her wrist.

"Where the hell did you get that?" he demanded.

Anna forced a smile and replied, "Jay Mizra gave it to me for Christmas. We're dating."

Her smile turned genuine when she saw her father rendered speechless. She knew he hated not knowing and controlling everything and everyone in his surroundings.

Oliver let out a disapproving grunt, and Anna shot him a mischievous wink. She fought back the laughter that threatened to erupt as the concern grew on his face.

Meredith, at least, was thrilled about the blossoming romance. Anna felt grateful she had someone to talk to about her growing feelings for Jay.

Presents were opened with little fanfare as Thomas' sullen mood permeated the room. At two-thirty, he turned the TV on, and while he and Oliver watched football, Anna and Meredith headed to the kitchen to heat the catered meal delivered the day before. The dining room table was beautifully set. The leaf had been removed so the table felt warmer and more conducive to a family dinner than a dinner party.

At three-thirty, Thomas came into the kitchen to see what was taking so long. Both Anna and her mom were annoyed he was rushing through such a special day; they both knew the reason why he wanted to be gone.

"Dinner will be on the table in fifteen minutes. Surely your mistress can wait. After all, she's been bought and paid for." Acid dripped from Meredith's voice.

Thomas' face flushed with anger. He turned on his heel and went back to the great room. Anna looked at her mom with raised eyebrows. Meredith shrugged and turned back to the oven, but her pain was palpable, and Anna's heart ached for her. Every year, Meredith wanted Christmas to be a special time, and every year, Thomas ruined it.

The table was overflowing with more food than they could ever eat. All her father's favorite holiday dishes were there. Anna and Oliver exchanged a glance over the centerpiece. Each knew what the other was thinking. Their mother kept trying to keep her marriage afloat while Thomas wanted nothing to do with his family. He just made the necessary appearances to keep neighbors and society members from talking.

Once everyone had filled a plate and grace was said, their father's mood darkened even more. After he had shoveled several forkfuls into his mouth, he decided to lash out at his target: Anna.

"I had a phone call Friday afternoon from the bank manager. The custodial account I was in charge of was removed from our bank. Who the hell do you think you are to take that money, and where is it?

Oliver gave Anna an encouraging look. She hated that she still felt a knot in her stomach whenever her father raised his voice at her.

She willed herself to look directly at him. "The account you are referring to was an UTMA, and according to Grandpa's will, it should have been transferred to me over a year ago. But you never saw fit to tell me about its existence. Mr. Milton moved the money to a new account in my name only. I chose to transfer it from the bank. A good decision, I think, since the bank manager had no legal right to inform you about money that belongs to me."

Thomas slammed his fist on the table. Everyone jumped at the sound, and the plates and cutlery rattled at his rage. "You are nothing but a gold-digging little bitch." His glare turned to Meredith. "I warned you not to take her into this house. She conned my father out of a million dollars that should have gone to me. She was unwanted when you adopted her, and as far as I'm concerned, that hasn't changed."

Meredith stood up and Anna followed suit. It was the latter who lashed out first. "You're an ignorant, narcissistic old man. I was three days old when Mom brought me home. How could I possibly have cared about your money? I was ten when Grandpa Cahill died. He left me that money because he loved me. If you want to see a greedy bastard, look in the mirror. You're the one who is unwanted in this house!"

Thomas' reaction was lightning fast. He stood up and punched Anna across the left side of her face, knocking her into the corner of the hutch before she hit the wood floor. Oliver immediately stood up and struck his father in the gut. Thomas fell backwards into the wall. Meredith dropped to the floor next to Anna to check on her unconscious daughter.

She looked up at her husband and screamed, "Get out! You disgust me! Don't ever set foot in this house again."

Thomas opened his mouth to sound off, but Oliver stepped in front of him. "Leave now," he told his father. His voice was low and threatening.

Thomas walked to the doorway and, in one last fit of rage, punched a hole through the drywall. He cried out as his fist found a solid wood beam, his hand breaking with an audible crack. Swearing, he grabbed his coat and slammed the door behind him.

Oliver joined his mother at Anna's side. "Mom, we need to call an ambulance. We can't protect Dad anymore."

Meredith, with tears streaming down her cheeks, nodded her agreement.

Within minutes, the police and EMTs arrived. Anna was transported to Evanston Hospital. The CT scan and MRI showed she had suffered a concussion, in addition to swelling and contusions along her left cheekbone and a lump the size of a large egg on the right side of her forehead. The doctor informed Meredith that she was lucky her daughter didn't have a brain bleed given the force with which she'd hit the solid wood credenza of the decorative cabinet.

Anna was kept well into the night for observation. Meredith insisted on sleeping in a chair beside her hospital bed, while Oliver returned home to clean up the mess left behind.

CHAPTER 15

March 12, 2017

Tension wound through Mike's body as he impatiently waited for Mizra to finish his meeting with the UAE consular representative. Sleep had been nonexistent last night, and the mixture of exhaustion and adrenaline was making him agitated. He could feel his heart pulsing in his ears. The pot of coffee he'd consumed that morning hadn't helped any.

After Kirkland stormed out following yesterday's failed interview, Harland, Mike and Kate had spent a few hours planning today's pass at Mizra. Harland had made it infinitely clear that if Mike and Kate couldn't put this to bed, they'd be reassigned to a field office in the middle of nowhere. By the time he got home, Mike was so keyed up that he'd paced the kitchen until the wee hours of the morning.

Mike startled at the sound of the door opening.

"Jeez, relax, Mike. It's just me," Kate chided. "Mizra and his rep are on their way up. Harland is in the viewing room now."

She waved at the mirrored wall and gave Mike a look across the table, away from Harland's view. After five years as partners, Mike read her cue loud and clear. Harland wouldn't be alone behind the glass; Kirkland would be watching every minute.

There was a single rap on the door before it opened. The consular representative entered first with Mizra following behind him. Kate noticed Mizra was no longer handcuffed. An agent stood guard outside the door.

"Good morning, I'm Omar Fadel from the UAE Embassy in New York." He shook Mike's hand and then Kate's.

After all introductions were made, the four of them were seated at the metal table. Another knock at the door brought a guard delivering four bottles of water. Mike took a long sip and waited for them to begin.

"As you are aware, Mr. Mizra was picked up on his way to the airport for a scheduled flight to his home country. At no time did your agents inform Mr. Mizra as to why he was taken against his will and placed in an FBI holding cell. Despite that gross injustice, Mr. Mizra has been docile and cooperated fully."

Kate could see Mike's leg shaking under the table. She decided to lead off. "Mr. Fadel, we informed Mr. Mizra as to why he had been detained and ended the interview as soon as he requested representation, pursuant to the Vienna Convention."

"You are holding a foreign national with no proof he committed a crime," Fadel stated emphatically.

"Three people, all from the same family, with which Mr. Mizra is closely associated, were murdered two days ago. A fourth member of the family was critically wounded. Mr. Mizra's personal driver, Aalam Barakat, identified as the assailant, was also dead at the scene. This gives us reasonable cause to hold Mr. Mizra for questioning."

"Is he under arrest?" Fadel asked.

Before either agent could answer there was a knock on the glass.

"Excuse us for just a moment."

Mike and Kate exited the room. Next door, Harland and Kirkland were waiting. Kate watched through the glass as Omar Fadel took out his cell phone and made a call.

"What are the odds that call is to a defense attorney?" she asked rhetorically.

Harland looked at Kirkland. "Well, Chief, how do you want to handle this? Everything we have is circumstantial, albeit damning."

Kirkland growled under his breath. "I can't authorize an arrest without something more concrete. No doubt he will be lawyered up by this afternoon. Let's bring the girl in to talk to him. See what he'll tell her. Just make sure she doesn't admit to witnessing the crime."

Mike started to interject, but Harland gave him a quick shake of his head. "Mike, call your agents and tell them to bring Anna Cahill in. Kate, go let them know Mizra is not under arrest, but we'd like him to wait around to speak to Ms. Cahill. She'll be here in less than an hour. If he's telling the truth about his affection for her, he won't pass up a chance to see her."

Harland looked at Kirkland to make sure he approved of his orders. Kirkland nodded and left the viewing room cursing.

While Mike called SA McCormack, Kate returned to the interview room.

"Mr. Mizra's attorney will be here within the hour," Fadel announced once Kate was seated.

She nodded. "Jahir Mizra is not under arrest at this time," she told him, then looked directly at Jay. "Mr. Mizra, Anna Cahill would like to meet with you. She is on her way to our office right now. It should be less than an hour if you are willing to see her, either with or without your attorney and consular representative."

Jay was desperate to see Anna, but held back his tears. "Is Anna ok?"

"Physically, Anna is fine. Emotionally, she is overwrought due to her family members' brutal deaths. Her one remaining family member is currently in the ICU."

Jay tried to speak, but his consular representative interjected. "Mr. Mizra will be happy to speak to Ms. Cahill when she arrives. We will wait here if that is agreeable."

"Of course. Can I get you coffee or something to eat while you are waiting?"

"Two coffees, and I'm sure you have some donuts around here somewhere," Fadel said sarcastically.

"I'll have an agent bring them in shortly," she replied politely, unwilling to acknowledge the representative's rude tone. She glanced at Jay. "I'll let you know as soon as Anna arrives."

"Thank you," he said sincerely. Kate was beginning to wonder if Harland's intuition was correct, if Jay really was shocked by the assassinations. "We'll let you know when your attorney arrives, too."

She left the room and asked an agent to get them what they requested.

CHAPTER 16

December 26, 2016

The light stabbed Anna's eyes through her closed lids. She groaned in pain and put her hand up, shielding her eyes as she opened them.

She was back in her bedroom. Vague memories of the hospital pressed against her, but it hurt too much to think.

Meredith delicately sat on the edge of her bed. "How are you doing, my angel?"

"It's too bright in here. Can you pull the shades?"

"Of course." She nodded to Oliver, who was hovering nearby. "Let's give you some pain medicine and something for the nausea. The doctor said it could take a few days for the worst of your symptoms to subside. It'll be at least two weeks for your concussion to be completely gone."

Once the room was darkened, Oliver gently helped Anna sit up, with several pillows behind her. She swallowed the medication gratefully.

"What happened? I can't remember."

"That's not unusual. Details will come back to you as your body rests and you have time to heal." Meredith spoke softly to her.

Anna gingerly touched her face and felt pain and swelling along the left side. Above her right eye was a large bump. "What the hell happened to my face? I need to see a mirror."

Oliver handed her a hand mirror from her dresser. "Our father happened," he answered bitterly.

Anna cried out at her reflection, seeing her bruised and swollen face. "This will take weeks to go away. How can I go back to school looking like this?"

"Honey, don't worry about school right now," Meredith told her. "You still have a couple weeks before classes resume. The most important thing for you to do is to rest. You need to eat, too. Let me go fix you something. Oliver will keep you company while I'm gone."

Oliver took his mother's place at Anna's bedside. She looked at him as directly as she could with light still pouring in from the openings around the shades. "Why did Dad do this?"

"He was angry you took control of your inheritance and moved it out of the bank." Oliver leaned in close. "I hope you transferred it to the offshore bank I recommended."

"I did. I do remember that. I received confirmation on Friday that the funds had been received."

Oliver sighed in relief.

"Where's my phone?" Anna asked.

"Mom has it. Who do you need to contact?" Oliver asked suspiciously.

"I have a date with Jay tomorrow. I can't go like this."

Meredith came around the corner with some dry toast. "Don't worry about Jay, I've already talked to him."

"What?" Anna and Oliver said in unison.

"Don't get snippy. Although the doctor did tell me the concussion could affect your personality."

She handed the plate to Anna, who could feel the bile rising just looking at the offering. She handed it back to her mom.

"No? Well, maybe later." Meredith smiled. "I wasn't being pushy. Jay kept texting your phone when we were at the hospital. He was concerned you weren't responding, so he called. I spoke to him briefly and filled him in. He was beside himself with worry. He caught the first flight this morning and is on his way here now to see you."

"Mom!" Anna started to panic. "He can't see me like this. I look hideous."

"Not to mention he'll probably fire us after seeing what the president of Cahill Investment Bankers did to his own daughter," Oliver added.

"Glad your heart is in your wallet, big brother."

"No, Anna, that's not what I meant. We all rely on income from the company. If word gets out Dad put his own daughter in the hospital, we'll lose a lot of clients. We can't afford that right now."

"Don't worry, Oliver. I'm not going to press charges against Dad. I'm too embarrassed for anyone to know that my father did this to me. I'm not eight years old anymore. Besides, Jay knows you are the one handling everything for him and I've told him how great you are. He won't fire you."

"Anna, I'm sorry. I didn't mean it to sound like I care more about the company than you. I punched Dad hard in the gut last night after he hit you."

"Seriously?"

"Yeah, he was so pissed he put his fist through the dining room wall, right into a stud. He broke his hand. I heard the crack." Oliver relished the memory.

"Thank you." Anna smiled at the thought.

The doorbell rang and Anna again felt her panic begin to rise.

"I'll get the door." Oliver got up and went downstairs.

"Sweetheart, don't worry," Meredith said. "Jay already knows you're beautiful. I think it says a lot about him that he rushed back here to be with you." She kissed her daughter's forehead and squeezed her hand.

A moment later, Jay and Oliver were standing in her doorway. Anna tried to turn the left side of her face toward the window so Jay wouldn't see it. Even with the shades down, the room was well lit.

Jay knelt by her bed. He found her hand and held it. Anna looked at him and then her family. Meredith took Oliver by the arm, and they left the room. She closed the door behind them.

"Anna, are you in pain? Of course you are. I'm stupid to even ask that. What can I do?" Jay's words came spilling out like a waterfall.

"Just the fact that you came here means a lot. I hate it, though, that you are seeing me this way."

Jay kissed her hand and then moved onto the bed next to her. "You're concerned about me seeing you injured? Don't be crazy! I didn't sleep at all last night. I was so worried about you. I'm going to protect you. No one is going to hurt you again. Especially not your father!" Anna could hear the anger in his voice.

She could no longer hold back the wall of tears. The full extent of her father's hatred for her overwhelmed her, and she started to sob. Jay lay down carefully beside her on the bed and pulled her toward him, making sure not to touch her injuries as he held her. He whispered in her ear, "Anna, I've got you."

They lay together until Anna, exhausted and feeling the effects of the sedative, fell asleep on his shoulder. Jay rested his cheek on the top of her head.

"I love you, Anna Cahill," he whispered, knowing she was sound asleep and couldn't hear him. He felt her warmth and the calm beating of her heart, and drifted off with her in his arms.

***

"Anna." Meredith gently touched her daughter's arm.

Anna opened her eyes and realized Jay was gone.

Her mother read the question in her eyes. "Jay is in the guest bedroom. He didn't want to leave you, but I told him to get some sleep."

Anna held her pounding head between her hands. "Can I have any more pain medication?"

"Yes, but you need to eat some of this chicken bouillon I made you. Your nausea will get worse with nothing in your stomach but painkillers."

Meredith helped Anna sit up, and put the tray across her lap. Anna swallowed her medication with some water and then took a sip of the broth.

"It tastes good, Mom. Thank you."

"I'm so sorry, Anna. This should never have happened. I should have left your father a long time ago." Meredith's eyes were brimming with tears.

"Mom, it's not your fault. I'm curious, though, why you're still with Dad. You're beautiful and refined. He's a bully and doesn't value you."

Meredith looked resigned. "I lost my parents in a car accident when Tommy was a toddler and Oliver was an infant. I had no family left except for your brothers and your father."

"How did you even meet Dad if you're from Greenwich? You went to undergrad and law school at the University of Connecticut."

Meredith gave a wry smile. "I was in my final year of law school. I had just been through a painful break up with my boyfriend of several years. My girlfriends took me out to cheer me up. Your dad happened to be at the same bar. One of his college friends had just relocated to Hartford, Connecticut."

"And you found him attractive?" Anna's question came out more abrasive than she meant it to.

Meredith laughed at her daughter's comment. "Thomas was funny, spontaneous and a little rough around the edges. He was the complete opposite of the man who had broken my heart. I figured I'd never hear from him again, but he called me after he got back to Chicago. He wanted to fly back to Hartford to see me. After six months of long-distance dating, he proposed. My parents weren't pleased. My family was old money—I had even been a debutante in my senior year of high school." She smiled at the memory. "I was expected to marry someone from the same station as me. My former boyfriend was my perfect match in that respect. We'd been together since our freshman year of college. I always thought we'd wed, and so did my parents. He broke up with me to marry someone a little higher up the society food chain."

"What a creep!" Anna was disgusted and angry at this man she didn't know for hurting her mother.

"I was devastated and humiliated. When your father pursued me so persistently, it was what I needed at the time. I'm not sure if I was really in love with Thomas or if he was just an escape from my very public heartbreak. That's one of the negatives of being amongst the wealthiest in society: There are no secrets, only gossip."

"What about your parents?"

"We kept in touch, but it was strained. I would visit them without your father. I'm glad they got to meet my sons before they passed. When I returned from their funeral, I was devastated. Your father, on the other hand, was furious when I told him I didn't receive my parents' estate, even as their only child. That's when I saw what my parents had always seen: Your father married me for the money he thought I would inherit. But it was too late. I'd lost everyone I loved except for my sons."

"Why did you stay with him?"

"Your father manages money for his livelihood, and I had barely begun to practice law. I couldn't practice as a single mother to two little ones. If I'm honest, I think there was some part of me that thought your dad loved me." She sighed, and looked across at Anna, a sad smile on her lips. "There is more I need to discuss with you, but I should probably let you rest." Meredith gave her daughter a kiss on her forehead.

As she started to walk out of the room, Anna called out to her, "Mom, you don't need him anymore. You have Oliver and me. We'll take care of you."

Meredith smiled. "I already spoke to an attorney this morning."

Anna's face mirrored her mother's sadness. She hated her father for his cruelty. "I love you, Mom."

She laid her head down on her pillow and was soon back asleep.

CHAPTER 17

March 12, 2017

Curtis Ballenger entered the interview room like he owned it. He sat opposite Jay and Omar, pulling a notebook and pen out of his briefcase. Ballenger was an imposing figure. He stood six feet four inches tall and had a muscular build. Omar nodded his head in approval of the attorney's impressive stature and commanding presence.

"Alright, let's have a discussion before they bring Ms. Cahill in to pull at your heartstrings," Ballenger said.

"Don't speak about her that way!" Jay's response was defensive.

Ballenger held his hands up. "Sorry. I don't mean to imply that your girlfriend is trying to pull one over on you. I do think they are using her as bait, with or without her knowledge."

Omar inclined his head in agreement. "My thoughts exactly."

Jay gave the representative a nasty look. He wasn't about to let these two men gang up on Anna.

"Ok, Jay, the microphone is off, so this room is soundproof," Ballenger said. "As your attorney, anything you tell me is privileged and I'm sworn not to reveal it without your express permission. I need to hear exactly what happened on March tenth. There is nothing I hate more than being caught with my pants down because my client failed to tell me something and the prosecution knows the score before I do."

Omar stepped in. "Excuse me, Mr. Ballenger. You may not be aware, but Mr. Mizra comes from one of the most respected families in Dubai. You need to speak to him accordingly."

Ballenger let out a frustrated sigh. "Mr. Fadel, it doesn't matter to me if Jahir Mizra is royalty or a truck driver, I treat all my clients the same. I'm the best damn defense attorney in Chicago and I'm here for you"—he turned to Jay as he spoke—"even if you don't like my style, and as long as I get paid." He grinned.

Jay had been in Chicago long enough to understand Ballenger was brusque by nature, not rude. "I'm glad you're here, Mr. Ballenger."

"Good! Now, tell me what you know about the Cahill murders."

"I only know what the FBI agents have told me."

"So, if I'm hearing you right, you had nothing to do with Mr. Barakat carrying out these assassinations?"

"That's correct. I was heading to the airport for a flight to Dubai I booked several weeks ago. I wasn't fleeing. Just the opposite. I was going back to prepare for my permanent move to Chicago. I don't even know who was killed."

Ballenger wrote down some notes on his pad before continuing. "I can answer that last part for you. Thomas, Meredith and David Cahill died at the scene. Oliver Cahill had a bullet tear through his femoral artery. The FBI is being very hush about his condition, but I have a friend at the hospital who confirmed Oliver went through a lengthy surgery and needed multiple transfusions."

Jay turned pale at this news.

"Let's start from your arrival in Chicago this past December. Did you call the car service to book Mr. Barakat as your driver for a six-month contract?"

"No." Jay was emphatic. "My father's secretary took care of the arrangements for me. She booked the driver, the hotel and even found a flat for me to lease once I determined I wanted to start my real estate business in Chicago."

Ballenger continued taking notes. "How did you come to work with Cahill Investment Bankers in pursuit of your commercial purchase?"

"My father recommended them based on their reputation among his business associates. Cahill has experience with international buyers. You need to realize, I came here to separate myself from my father's business. We had different... beliefs and business tactics. He agreed to provide me with a monetary gift to get started in the US."

"Can you think of any reason your father would hire Barakat to assassinate the Cahill family?" Ballenger looked directly at Jay. "Whatever you tell me doesn't leave this room."

Jay looked at Ballenger and then at Omar Fadel, who appeared very interested in the conversation.

"Omar, please leave the room."

Omar protested that he needed to stay as the consular representative, but Ballenger dismissed him with a wave of his hand. Omar got up from the table with an indignant look.

"We'll call you back when we need you," Ballenger said. "Take the opportunity to stretch your legs, get some lunch." Once the door slammed behind Omar, he turned to Jay. "Are you worried Mr. Fadel might report back to your father?"

"It's hard to say. My father has undue influence over a great many people in Dubai and I'm sure he has spies at the embassy here."

"Why don't you tell me more about your father?" Ballenger flipped to a new page in his notepad.

"My father and brother-in-law are Hamas sympathizers. For several years, after I returned from England, they kept me insulated from their 'charitable' activities. About a year ago, I inadvertently overheard a phone call regarding delivery of US military arms to the terrorist group. I did some checking and discovered my father was funding the purchases through the company's profits. I didn't confront my father because I knew I'd be killed. He and my brother-in-law are hardcore. Instead, I approached him with a business plan to build my own company in the United States."

Jay stopped and took a drink of water. A combination of fear and tension was flowing through his body, but he knew he had to tell his attorney his theory.

"Go on when you are ready." Ballenger softened his tone.

"The start-up money my father gave me wasn't a gift. He and my brother-in-law were buying me out of my share in the company. I was receiving a fraction of what I was owed, but it was enough. I wanted to get away from them and any affiliation with their business as quickly as possible."

"So, you got away unscathed. How do you explain the murders?"

"About three weeks ago, I received a call from my father. It was the first time I'd heard from him since I left Dubai. My father isn't a sentimental man, so I knew it wasn't a friendly call. He was angry. He didn't know I already knew about the weapons. He was desperate for information and needed me to get it. Someone had tipped off his military supplier about an FBI investigation into arms smuggling. His supplier got spooked and backed out, leaving my father empty-handed. Not something you want to be when you've made promises to Hamas."

"What did you tell him?"

Jay's heart was beating fast, and he could see Ballenger's own tension in the line of his shoulders. "I told him the truth—I had no idea what he was talking about. That's when he told me Cahill Investment Bankers was also under investigation by the FBI. Apparently, they had worked with foreign clients restricted by the US government. I reminded him that I went to Cahill Investment Bankers on his recommendation. He informed me the FBI had been surveilling me since my arrival. I was shocked."

"You really had no idea?" Ballenger was incredulous.

"See, that's exactly why I didn't approach the FBI. I knew they'd think I was trying to cut a deal. I had nothing to offer them. I still don't know who my father's contact in the government is. I'm involved purely because of my last name."

"What I'm hearing is you suspect your father arranged the murders to squash the investigation into the Cahills. You think he was afraid one of their clients would lead back to him. Is that accurate?"

"Yes, but I don't know any of the players in this whole scenario. Everything Oliver and I did to purchase the hotel was above board. We had begun work on finding my next property. I love Anna Cahill and want a life with her. Why would I murder her family?" Jay flushed with frustration.

"The good news, for you, is there is nothing linking you to the murders. It would help if you had the name of the traitor who is selling military-grade weapons to your father."

"I have no idea!" Jay was getting angry. "Like I said, the only reason I'm here is my last name."

"What exactly were the loose ends you needed to tie up in Dubai?"

"Put my house up for sale and pack up personal belongings to ship to my new address here in Chicago. I also wanted to see my mother one last time. I knew once I left Dubai, I would never go back."

"You weren't afraid of your father or brother-in-law?"

"My father is a cruel man but he's very intelligent. If his son disappeared or turned up dead during an ongoing investigation, he would be putting himself in the spotlight."

Ballenger sat back in his seat, flipping his pen through his fingers as he read through his notes. His silence had Jay jumping out of his skin.

"Well?" Jay asked him. "What do you recommend?"

"I think the best thing to do is tell the FBI everything you just told me. We'll demand immunity first, of course."

"But I don't know anything!"

"Yes, Jay, you do. You know your father and brother-in-law are buying US military weapons from a member of the US government who knows full well who the final recipient of said weapons will be. You also know the FBI has a mole who tipped off the supplier. Just because you don't have any names doesn't make your information any less valuable. I'm going to have a discussion with the chief federal prosecutor and see if we can get immunity. Until then, you say nothing, not even to Mr. Fadel."

"What about Anna? She should be here any minute." Jay's face lit up and then fell just as quickly when his attorney shook his head.

"No contact, no conversation with anyone until I come back with a letter of immunity from the chief. Got it?"

Jay nodded, but his eyes filled with tears. Anna was so close, but he couldn't touch her or console her. He hoped she didn't think he was involved.

"Don't worry, I'll let them know that no one enters this room until I come back. You stay put and stay quiet." Curtis Ballenger stood up and left to find Kirkland.

CHAPTER 18

December 27, 2016

Anna could hear voices coming from downstairs. She gingerly put on her robe and held the banister as she descended the back stairs into the kitchen.

"What are you doing?" Oliver scolded when he saw her. "You should be in bed!"

"I can't stay in bed all day. The doctor told me to rest; he didn't specify it had to be alone in my room."

Meredith smiled at her daughter's stubbornness. They may not have been biologically related, but there was something about nurture over nature. "Oliver, pull out a chair for her. Anna, how about scrambled eggs and toast?"

To her surprise, she was feeling hungry. "Thanks, Mom. That would be great."

"Anna!" Jay entered the kitchen, smiling. He was fresh from the shower and holding his phone. "I apologize. I had to make a couple of calls this morning to let my team know I hadn't been abducted," he joked.

"You're just in time, Jay," said Meredith. "I'm making scrambled eggs and toast."

"Sounds great!" Jay poured himself a mug of coffee and retrieved a Coke from the refrigerator for Anna before sitting next to her. "How's the patient today?" Concern crossed his features as he examined her face.

"Ugly! That's how she is," Anna answered, frustrated.

Jay cupped her chin and kissed her unbruised cheek. "You are always beautiful to me."

Oliver, standing behind Jay, rolled his eyes to Anna. She ignored him and took a sip of her drink.

Meredith approached the table holding a plate laden with food for their guest. "Jay, I hope you don't mind being caught up in family discussion, but I want you all to know that my petition for divorce will be filed by the end of this week. Oliver, I'm sorry if this makes things difficult for you at work."

Anna looked at Oliver. She knew he would prefer never to set foot in Cahill Investment Bankers again, but he had to because of the FBI investigation. He caught her glance and, barely noticeably, shook his head—a warning not to mention anything.

"I think Thomas will stay far away from Oliver after the gut punch my brother delivered Christmas night." Anna was proud of him.

"So, he's 'Thomas' now?" Oliver asked with a smile.

"You don't really expect me to call him 'Dad' anymore, do you?"

Jay jumped in. "Oliver, did you really punch your father?"

Oliver nodded.

Jay reached over and shook his hand. "Excellent! I only wish I had been there to defend you as well," he said to Anna.

Anna could see Oliver bristle. He didn't care for the quickly growing affection between his sister and Jay Mizra. *When will he see how good Jay is to me?*

Meredith positioned herself across the table from Anna and reached for her hand. "Honey, when you feel up to it, my attorney will want to take your deposition. You too, Oliver. Thomas doesn't know it yet, but he is going to lose his shirt, and everything else!"

"Don't worry about the business, Jay," Oliver was quick to interject. "We'll continue as we have been, and all of your needs will be met."

"My business will remain with you," Jay assured him. "I responded to an email from your father this morning informing him that I'll only work with you."

"He emailed you?" Oliver's face flushed with anger.

"Yes, I believe it was damage control. He wanted to ensure that he would personally oversee my file. Not to worry, I was explicit in my response."

Oliver was suddenly concerned his father would try the same with all his clients. He inhaled his eggs, grabbed his coffee and headed to the study.

"Where are you going, dear?" Meredith called after him.

"I need to contact my entire client list. If Dad contacted Jay, he'll likely contact everyone else I work with." The study door slammed behind him.

Oliver's first call was to Mike Mallory. He needed to update the FBI as to the events over the past few days.

"Mallory." Mike was on autopilot. He'd just returned from a road trip with his wife to visit family in Minnesota, and was still trying to recuperate.

"Mike, it's Oliver. The holidays were a shitstorm at the Cahill house."

Mike put his coffee down and stood up at his desk. "Hold on, Oliver. I'm going to put you on speakerphone so Kate can get the update too." He signaled to Kate to follow him into a conference room and shut the door behind them. "Ok, we're both listening."

Oliver told him what his father had done to Anna and the subsequent fallout. There was stunned silence on the line.

"I can reassure you that Jay Mizra will remain as my client," Oliver told them.

"Did he call you and tell you that?" Kate asked.

"No, he's staying at our family home. He flew back early from Miami when he heard Anna was in the hospital. He told us at breakfast that my father tried to poach him."

"What? Mizra is staying with you?" Mike raised his voice in disbelief.

Oliver lowered his so no one would hear him outside the study doors. "Yes, just for a day or two until Anna is more improved. They are very attached to each other." His annoyance was obvious.

Kate could see Mike was about to pop off so she interjected. "Oliver, is this the first time your father has abused one of you?"

"Anna is the only one he ever abused. This is the second time requiring medical care. Other times it was bruises and welts. Trust me, my father will never set foot in this house again. My mother is filing for divorce this week."

"I'm so sorry your sister has had to go through this." Kate was visibly upset. "It's good your mother is divorcing him."

"So long as it doesn't disrupt the company's clientele," Mike chimed in.

"Jeez, Mike! Can you be just a little more sympathetic for what this family is going through?" Kate was angry.

Mike put his hand up to silence her. Clearing his throat, he said, "I'm sorry, Oliver—I'm not trying to be a jerk, but you understand the importance of business as usual until we nail Mizra."

"I do and I'm on it."

"Don't lose focus!" Mike snapped. "Make sure your sister's relationship with Mizra ends when she goes back to college!"

"How do you propose I do that? She's an adult," Oliver responded, agitated.

"It's your job to figure it out. Keep us posted. I'm sure there will be some fallout we have to clean up." Mike disconnected the call.

Kate stood staring at him.

"What?" he asked, defensively.

"Sometimes, you're a real jackass, Mallory." She opened the door to the conference room and left him standing there.

CHAPTER 19

December 29, 2016

"Anna?" She heard her mother calling her.

"I'm just getting out of the shower. I'll be right there." Anna pulled on her sweatshirt and sweatpants and ran a brush through her freshly washed hair. When she walked into her bedroom, she found her mother perched on her bed with an anxious look on her face.

"Mom, is everything ok?"

"Yes. How are you feeling?" Meredith asked, eyeing her daughter's bruising and the knot on her head.

"I feel better. Taking a shower always helps." She smiled.

"If you're up to it, I'd like for us to go into my office and discuss a few things." Her mother's expression was serious. It made her nervous.

She tried not to show it. "Of course, let's go."

They walked down the hall to her mother's home office, and Meredith closed the door behind them. She motioned for Anna to take a seat next to her desk, then turned on her computer and printer.

"Mom, what's going on?"

"Anna, I lied to your father when I said my parents didn't leave me an inheritance. After the funeral, their attorney gave me a sealed letter. When I opened it, I found a statement for a Swiss bank account containing fifteen million dollars. It was meant for me and my children. I wasn't to tell Thomas about it. To be honest, after his reaction when I said my parents' estate went to my cousins, I didn't care to share the rest of my news." Meredith pulled up the account information and printed it out. She handed it to her daughter.

"Why are you giving me this?" Anna was confused.

"I've never touched this account. It has been sitting and accruing interest for almost thirty years. This is your inheritance, but you need to keep it a secret between us."

"What about Oliver?" Anna felt guilty getting this much money without her brother receiving half.

"After Tommy passed, your father and I redid our will, making Oliver the sole beneficiary. When we adopted you, I wanted to add a codicil providing an equal amount to you. Your father refused. I'm ashamed to say you will receive nothing from our estate."

"You don't think Oliver would give me anything?" Anna couldn't believe he'd leave her out in the cold.

"Don't get me wrong, I love Oliver with all my heart. He is very much like your father, however, and won't part with a dime of his inheritance."

"That doesn't sound like him, Mom," Anna protested.

"A couple of years ago, I would have agreed with you. Since he began working for Cahill Investments, he has changed quite a bit. He's more cutthroat, like your father, when it comes to business. It was his idea to expand into the foreign market. He asked me to set up shell companies for the overseas clientele. I did so without realizing some of them were on the OFAC list. Your father, brother and uncle trapped me."

Anna felt dizzy. She couldn't believe what she was hearing.

Oliver had lied about everything.

"So," Meredith continued, "keep this bank account a secret and don't lose the account number. No names were used in setting it up. I'd suggest you combine it with your grandfather's inheritance. I'm guessing Oliver gave you an offshore bank to deposit it in."

Anna nodded slowly, still reeling from the shock of what she'd just learned.

"I'm sorry to dump all this information on you, especially when you're recovering. I just want to make sure you are cared for if anything ever happens to me. I know you love your brother, but he's not the same Oliver you remember."

Meredith grabbed her hand and squeezed it. "Anna, you deserve the best and I think you have found yourself a keeper with Jay." She redirected the conversation with a smile. "Now, go get back in bed and I'll bring you up some lunch."

As Anna walked back down the hall, she felt a sudden wave of anger toward Oliver. He had lied to her and made Meredith out to be the villain, and he was going to get full immunity from the federal government.

She had to find a way to protect her mother. Anna carefully folded the account printout and put it in an inside zipper compartment of her backpack.

***

Anna was settled back in her bed, waiting for her mother to bring her lunch. She was at a loss as to what to do about Oliver. He had played her, but she was afraid to confront him. He had Meredith trapped, and Anna didn't even know who she could turn to. Anything she did, her mother would be prosecuted.

She was lost in her thoughts when Meredith showed up with a tray of toasted cheese, grapes and a glass of water. She set the tray in front of Anna and then sat down on the bed.

Anna looked at her expectantly.

Meredith gave a wry smile. "There is something else I need to tell you, but I'd like you to keep it between us."

Anna had a mouth full of toasted cheese, but she nodded emphatically.

"Next week, I'm having hidden security cameras with sound installed inside the house. I wanted you to know, but please, this must remain between us. Don't tell Oliver. I'm afraid he's in your father's pocket and would report back to him."

Anna slowly took in everything her mother had just told her.

"Are you scared to stay here alone, Mom?"

"No. I'm concerned once your father is served with the divorce complaint he will come back. I don't know what he has locked in his desk drawers in the study, but I don't think it would be to my benefit for him to retrieve anything. If Oliver knew, he might tell his father. Despite his dislike for Thomas, he still craves praise from him."

"Where are you going to put the system so no one sees it?" Anna was curious.

"The installers will take care of hiding the cameras and microphones to give me coverage of the front entry, study, my bedroom and my office. As for the hardware, they will set that up in the closet of the media room. That room rarely gets used. Christmas Eve was the first time Oliver set foot in there since last year. I don't remember your father ever using that room."

"I think you're smart, Mom. Dad is manipulative but he wouldn't be able to talk his way out of breaking and entering if it's recorded. Did your attorney file the temporary restraining order?"

"Yes, he did it yesterday. Your father can't come within a hundred yards of me or our house. At least not legally." Meredith grimaced.

Anna reached over her tray and put her hand on her mother's shoulder. "Mom, it'll be okay. You're doing everything right."

Meredith stood up and kissed her daughter's forehead. "Thank you. Now make sure you finish your lunch. Put the tray on the floor when you're done and try and get some sleep. I'll sneak in later and grab it." She paused in the doorway. "I love you, Anna. I'm sorry if I seem hard on you sometimes. I just want the best of everything for you."

Anna smiled. "I know, and I love you too, Mom."

***

Anna was just waking from a nap when she heard voices downstairs. Before she had time to get out of bed, Jay was standing in her doorway with an overnight bag.

"I thought you had work to do back in the city," she said, surprised.

"I finished up early. Your mom invited me to stay through the New Year so I could spend it with you."

Anna smiled sheepishly. "You do realize she is doing everything she can to further our relationship?"

"I do and I'm grateful!" He beamed. "Do you feel up for a movie in the media room? I'll grab your pillow and your blanket."

Anna nodded.

They settled into a double recliner, and Anna soaked in Jay's warmth as she snuggled in close.

"Thank you," she said, looking up at him.

"For?" Jay looked at her quizzically.

"Being here and making me feel safe."

Jay wrapped his arm around Anna and kissed her head.

Meredith stopped by with drinks and snacks before the movie started. She smiled as she closed the door behind her.

CHAPTER 20

February 10, 2017

Anna was overwhelmed with emotions as she made her way to baggage claim at Salt Lake City International Airport. Initially, excitement had ruled when Jay asked to fly her out to Park City for a ski weekend to celebrate Valentine's Day—her best friend, Sophie, took her shopping at an upscale lingerie store for the trip. Now, insecurities were settling in. She'd only had one serious boyfriend and that had been in her sophomore year of college. When she made the decision to quit cheerleading to dedicate more time to her academics, he quit her. She realized too late he'd liked the idea of dating a college cheerleader, not her as an individual. Since then, she had ignored guys to get her grades up for law school. Jay was the first to turn her head in almost two years. She didn't care he was ten years older than her, but it bothered her that he had a lot more romantic experience than she did.

"Anna!" Jay called out as she reached the baggage carousel. He was holding a bouquet of purple hydrangeas. Anna gave him a big hug and pushed down her fears for the moment.

"How did you know hydrangeas are my favorite flowers?" She was bewildered.

"You mentioned it when we were at the Christmas party. You said you hated poinsettias and wished people decorated with hydrangeas year-round."

Anna smiled up at Jay. She couldn't believe he'd remembered. *She* didn't even remember that.

She pointed out her bag and he grabbed it off the moving track, laughing at the size and heft of it.

"What?" she asked defensively. "Ski clothes take up a lot of room!" Jay made a face at her, and she laughed. "Fine, I'm an over-packer. I admit it."

Soon they were in the warm SUV on their way to the house Jay had rented. He was excited because it was ski-in/ski-out. He had grown up skiing in Switzerland and Austria. She'd only skied twice in her life, once at Lake Louise in Canada and the other time in Taos, New Mexico.

"Are you going to leave me on the bunny hill while you go ski black diamonds?" Anna joked as she cuddled him.

"Absolutely not, but we are going to start on the greens. You've got a couple of ski trips under your belt; I think you're underestimating your ability. I can't wait for you to see the house. It's beautiful. I have people there now cooking dinner for us—I figured you would be starving."

"Seriously? You hired people to make us dinner?" Anna was amazed by his thoughtfulness.

"Yes, but I expect you to make the porridge in the morning." He smiled and leaned in to kiss her. She never got tired of the butterflies she felt every time.

Jay closed the window behind the driver for more privacy. Anna felt a trickle of nerves. Obviously, the driver could see through the glass, but he couldn't hear their conversation. What could Jay have to say?

"What's up?" she asked.

"When we were talking last night, you seemed a little distant. I want to make sure you're totally comfortable on this trip. I don't have any expectations of you, if you know what I mean." It was Jay's turn to be nervous.

Anna nodded and held his hands in hers. "The thing is, I've only had one real boyfriend. You've dated beautiful models and actresses. I guess... I feel like I might disappoint you."

"Anna, you are incomparable. I'm happy you don't have a lot of experience in that way. I wish I had been more discerning when I was younger. There's no pressure. If you just want to lie on the couch together and watch movies at night, I'm fine with that. I just want to be with you and sleep next to you."

This time, Anna leaned in and kissed Jay deeply. She felt a lot more than butterflies as he returned her kiss with intensity.

***

After dinner, they sat outside in front of the fire pit and sipped brandy together. The moonlight reflected off the snow, making the skyline bright. Anna relished the happiness she felt with Jay's arm around her, listening to the fire crackle and the deep hoot of the great horned owl. It took her a moment to realize he was a little restless.

Anna sat up and faced him, concerned. "Is something wrong?"

"No, it's not that. I'm not very good sometimes at saying what I'm thinking."

"So far, you've been a great communicator."

He returned her smile, but quickly turned serious again. "I'm afraid I'm going to scare you off because we only met two months ago. Maybe it's because I'm older, but I know what I want and it's you. I realize it's a lot to ask for us to be exclusive, but to be honest, I can't stand the thought of you seeing anyone else. I'd go crazy."

Anna smiled so hard her cheeks hurt. She wanted to remember the look of adoration in Jay's eyes forever. "I'm yours. Just yours," she replied.

He stood up and let out a whoop of excitement.

Anna started laughing. "Hush! You'll wake the neighbors. Now, your exclusive squeeze is freezing. I'm going to go take a shower. Meet you on the couch for a movie?"

Jay kissed her in response and helped her up off the bench.

As Anna stood in the shower, she felt elated. When she emerged from the bathroom, she sorted through her suitcase, looking for one item. It was a black lace chemise.

She put her cinched cotton robe over it and then opened the bedroom door. Jay was lying on the couch in a long-sleeved T-shirt and sweatpants. He smiled as she entered the room.

Anna walked to the edge of the couch and slid off her robe.

CHAPTER 21

March 12, 2017

Mike Mallory's internal fuel gauge was empty when he was summoned to Jack Harland's office. He entered the room to find Harland sitting on the wrong side of his own desk, and the chief federal prosecutor in his chair.

"C'mon in, Mike." Harland motioned him to take a seat in the corner. "We are waiting for Mizra's attorney, Curtis Ballenger, to join us. He called this little meeting. Kirkland and I thought you should be present since you've been running with this case for months."

Discomfort settled over him like a cloud. There was only one reason Ballenger would want to meet, and that was to cut a deal.

Mike looked at his physical position in the room: well out of the way of the desk, and clearly at the bottom of the authoritative food chain.

Ballenger knocked as he opened the door. *He's got balls*, Mike thought. *He can't even wait for permission to enter a closed office.* Harland noticed Mike's look of disdain and slightly raised his hand, a signal he'd used multiple times before. Mike was to stand down and just listen.

Ballenger's size was imposing, and his manner was abrupt. "Gentlemen, I want you to give my client immunity."

"That's not even an 'ask,'" Kirkland scoffed. "Why don't you try sitting down and telling us why he deserves it?" He pointed to the chair next to Harland.

Ballenger turned the chair so he was facing all three of the men.

"He's not under arrest. You have no evidence linking him to any illegal activity and you can't keep him from flying back to Dubai. If you try, there may well be an international incident with the UAE. His consular representative is filing a complaint that the FBI held a member of one of Dubai's most respected families for twenty-four hours with no explanation and no contact with his embassy."

Harland laughed quietly to himself.

"You find that funny? As the SSA of this field office, I would think you'd be begging to make a deal with me." Ballenger pointed to Kirkland. "Do you think this guy is going to take the heat? No, sir. He's going to blame this travesty on you and your agents."

"Well." Harland straightened in his chair. "If he is as innocent and mistreated as you say, why does he need a deal?"

"My client was not involved and had no knowledge of the Cahill murders, either before or after they were carried out. In fact, he was shocked when SA DeSoto told him about them in his initial interview. Did I mention that was twenty-four hours after he was incarcerated with no explanation?"

"Stop your damn lawyering and get to the point!" Kirkland's irritation at his posturing was contagious. Mike moved to the edge of his chair.

Ballenger nodded. "Hypothetically, if my client had information regarding the incident in question, which he didn't realize was pertinent until after the shootings took place, he would share those details with you under a written statement of full immunity. Approved by me first, of course."

Mike's temper flared. "That's a long fucking way of admitting he's withholding information."

"Mike." Harland silenced him with a glare.

Ballenger smiled at the beleaguered SA.

"You'd need to be more specific, Mr. Ballenger, before the US is going to grant immunity to a foreign national who is conducting business on our soil while on the OFAC blacklist."

Kirkland tapped his fingers together, not breaking eye contact with the attorney.

Ballenger visibly enjoyed his work. "For starters, Mr. Mizra had no idea he was on the OFAC list. I don't believe you notify individuals by email or snail mail when they make the list."

His sarcasm had Mike shifting in his seat. He wanted nothing more than to deck the smug bastard.

"Let's assume my client has information that would greatly advance your investigation into who is selling US military-grade weapons to hostiles and perhaps even reveal the mole you have here at the Federal Bureau of Investigation." Ballenger's smile was cocky.

Mike cursed in his head. He knew Kirkland would go for the immunity deal if it meant getting traitors into the federal frying pan.

Kirkland let the room sit in silence for several uncomfortable minutes. Mike noticed Harland shifting in his chair, but Ballenger kept the same "eat shit" grin on his face. The punk was completely unfazed.

Finally, the chief prosecutor broke the silence. "Mr. Mizra would have to work with the US government to get evidence against the treasonous individuals and help implicate the foreigners purchasing the weapons. If he is willing to do that, he gets immunity. If he fails, he becomes an accomplice." Kirkland stared at Ballenger, waiting for him to flinch.

Ballenger slapped his hand on the arm of the chair and stood up. "Give me ten minutes to confer with my client and I'll let you know if we have a deal." He exited the office, leaving the door open. Mike stood and slammed it behind him.

"Keep your cool, Mallory," Kirkland chided. "Do you think Mizra's guilty?"

"My instinct is no, but I don't like his attorney trying to strong-arm us."

Harland nodded his agreement. "If he agrees to the terms, this might work to our advantage," he added.

Kirkland started throwing out ideas on how to utilize Mizra as a spy. The conversation was cut short when Ballenger gave a quick knock and opened the door.

"Draw it up. If I like the way it sounds, he'll sign it. Oh, and he wants to see the girl." Ballenger smiled. "Love doing business with the US government!" He chuckled as he walked down the hall.

Kirkland looked at Mike. "Is the girl here yet?"

Mike nodded.

"Get her in there. You and Harland watch them, while I draft this damn agreement."

CHAPTER 22

March 12, 2017

The starkness of the interview room left Anna unsettled, with its cold, metal table and two-way mirror. She had been brought to the FBI field office with no explanation from the special agent babysitting her that day. She sipped her Coke, hoping it would help settle her nerves, and released an audible sigh of relief when the door opened and Kate DeSoto and Mike Mallory walked in. Each took a seat across the table.

"Why am I here?"

"SA Moreno didn't fill you in?" Kate was surprised. Mike gently kicked her under the table.

"Anna, we wanted to give you an update," he said.

Anna looked at him with suspicion. "No, you wouldn't drive me from Naperville to downtown Chicago for an update. Something is going on, and I deserve to know."

She was exhausted and angry at being kept away from her brother and in the dark.

"You're right," Mike apologized. "We were going to have you talk to Jay and see if he would open up to you. Right now, however, his attorney has barred anyone from seeing him."

"Jay is here?" There was a trace of panic in Anna's voice.

Mike looked at the young woman before him and cursed himself for agreeing to the planned meeting. He could see the toll the past few days had taken on her. Anna's eyes were swollen from crying and lack of sleep. She'd been left on pins and needles with no answers.

"Anna, I'm sorry we haven't been more forthcoming with you. After you identified Jay's driver, Aalam Barakat, as the shooter, we went to his apartment to look for evidence of who may have hired him to kill your family. We came up empty-handed. Mr. Mizra denies any knowledge of the murders. Our supervisors thought it might help retrieve important information if he could talk to you. Honestly, we don't know what to make of the situation at this point." Mike was as candid as he could be.

"What about Oliver? No one at the house will let me call him or take me to see him. I need to see him!"

"Oliver is recovering well, and he is under twenty-four-hour guard. At this point, we don't want to put either of you at further risk. Having you in a room together could be dangerous to you both until we know who ordered the assassination of your family," Kate explained gently.

Anna was desperate. "You don't understand! I need to talk to Oliver. I received some information yesterday that I need to tell him."

"What are you talking about?" Mike asked.

Kate looked just as confused as her partner.

"Oliver gave me one of those DNA genealogy kits for Christmas. He had taken an identical one a couple of years ago. He knew I was curious about my birth parents, and he thought this might help. I received an email from the company yesterday telling me I had a half-sibling." Anna's eyes filled with tears.

"That sounds like it's good news. Why are you upset?" Kate asked

"Because my half-sibling is Oliver Cahill," Anna choked out and the floodgates opened. She could hardly breathe; she was crying so hard.

Kate pulled her chair around next to Anna and held her.

Anna was gasping, trying to speak through her tears. "I need to tell Oliver. He's going to get the same email. Do you understand what this means?" She grabbed a handful of tissues to wipe her eyes and blow her nose.

Kate looked at Mike across the table. Simultaneously, it dawned on them.

"Oh my God, Thomas Cahill was your biological father," Mike said, stunned.

Anna sobbed harder. She'd had so many questions going through her head since she received the news. She needed to talk with Oliver.

"Meredith must have known when she adopted you," Mike said, thinking aloud.

"You think?" Anna's reply was caustic. Kate pulled her closer. "I'm sorry," she said. "I don't mean to be rude, it's just a lot to take in on top of everything else. I can't ask either of my parents why they adopted me. The thought of that animal being my real father makes me sick!"

Mike exhaled loudly and wiped his hand across his mouth. What the hell was going on in this family?

He stood up and addressed Kate. "Bring her in to see Jahir. I'll work on a visit to the hospital."

"Can I take one of my anxiety pills?" Anna asked.

Kate looked at this poor, bereft girl and her heart broke for her. She was anxious herself, and she was a trained agent. This mess was growing by the second.

"Sure, go ahead," she said. "Then we'll go to the ladies' room, and you can put some cold water on your face before we go see Mr. Mizra."

CHAPTER 23

March 12, 2017

Jay stood up when the door opened, and Anna hesitantly appeared. He crossed the room to hug her, but she stood with her arms at her sides.

"Anna, I promise I didn't have anything to do with this. They believe me." He waved toward the window. "I need to know you believe me."

Ballenger had insisted on staying in the room. He didn't want his client to risk his immunity. On the other side of the glass, Harland was having fits because of the lawyer's presence.

"Why don't you have a seat, young lady?" Ballenger motioned across the table from him and Jay.

Anna took a chair. She could feel no emotion left in her body.

"Anna, my father and brother-in-law must have been the ones to hire Barakat," Jay said. "You know I had my ticket to Dubai weeks ago. We talked about it. Do you remember?"

Anna nodded, and looked at him blankly. "Why would your father kill my family? Am I next?"

"I don't think so. I believe he was trying to stop the FBI investigation into Cahill Investment Bankers. He told me the FBI had been following me since I arrived in Chicago."

"What?" Anna perked up. Oliver had known Jay was a suspect but never bothered to mention it to her!

Jay reached across the table and grabbed her hands. She looked at his hands and felt the warmth. "Anna, I'm so sorry about what happened. I love you. I would never hurt you or hurt your family."

Anna studied his face. "I know you love me, but how are you going to stop your father or your brother-in-law? They're in Dubai."

"Mr. Mizra can't discuss that." Ballenger stood up. "I think we're done here."

"No!" Jay snapped. "Please, can you give us a few more minutes? I know everyone is watching through the glass. She's fine with me. I'll protect her."

Ballenger sighed and shrugged his shoulders. "You have ten minutes. I'll be in the next room observing. If you hear me knock on that glass, you shut your mouth." He pointed to Jay as he left the room.

Jay turned to Anna, his eyes full of hope. "Do you still love me?"

"Yes," Anna answered softly and squeezed Jay's hands.

He closed his eyes in relief.

Anna leaned in and spoke quietly. "They are going to take me away from you, from Oliver. I'm going to be all alone somewhere."

A knock on the window marked Ballenger's displeasure that he couldn't hear Anna.

Jay stood up and leaned over until he was speaking directly in Anna's ear. "I'm free. They gave me immunity. Don't worry—I'll find you, wherever you are. I promised I would protect you."

Ballenger opened the door and grabbed Mizra by the arm. "Time to go, buddy." He looked at Anna. "We're done here."

He pulled his client out the door and let it slam behind him.

Mike and Kate watched as Anna folded herself into a ball on the chair, as she had the first time they spoke with her. This time, however, there were no tears, no sobs. Just quiet.

CHAPTER 24

March 12, 2017

The elevator doors opened, and Anna stepped into the hall. A quick look to her left told her exactly where Oliver's room was located; the FBI agents didn't exactly blend into the woodwork. Kate and Mike walked quickly behind her trying to catch up, but she was at a full run by the time she reached her brother's door. One of the agents grabbed Anna's arm, causing her to unleash a tirade of words he would need a thesaurus to interpret.

Kate caught up to her first. "Nelson, let her in. She's the patient's sister."

The door swung open, and Anna rushed inside. Oliver cried tears of joy when he saw her unharmed. She leaned in gently to hug him. Gingerly, he moved over and Anna let the bedrail down so she could lie next to him. She put her head on his chest and cried out of grief and relief at finally seeing her brother.

Mike closed the door for privacy, and he and Kate stood over by the window, out of the way but not out of earshot.

Oliver started to tell Anna what had happened on Friday, but she sat up and looked at him. "I was there. I saw you and Barakat fighting."

"What? How were you there? You were supposed to be in Aruba." Oliver's words were coming fast and tinged with anger.

"I got my letter from Northwestern. I was coming home to tell you and Mom. I went in the side door and up the back staircase. When I heard the yelling, I crawled out onto the balcony and hid. I saw you get shot."

Oliver was visibly agitated. "You're lucky you didn't get hurt." His eyes flashed with irritation. He looked at the two agents. "Can Anna and I have a few minutes alone? A little privacy?"

Mike shook his head. "Sorry, Oliver. You two shouldn't even be in the same room. We can't leave you alone."

Oliver glared at the detective and then softened his gaze. "I'm sorry. The pain makes me irritable. I just wanted a few minutes to be alone with my sister and grieve."

Kate's gentle voice filled the room. "We understand, Oliver. It's just not allowed. Not now, with the investigation ongoing."

"I thought Barakat was dead. What else is there to investigate?"

"We can't discuss that with you right now. Anna, we only have a few minutes."

Anna caught the hint, but she was worried. "Why are you angry at me, Oliver?"

Oliver hesitated a moment. "I'm not angry," he huffed. "I just wish you hadn't been there. It's not something you should've seen."

"How are you doing?" Anna asked, looking at the leads attached to his chest and the IVs.

She was stalling, putting off showing Oliver the email. He was in a foul mood; she didn't know how he would react to such a shocking revelation.

"Better. The doctors saved my life. Hopefully, I'll be out of here by Tuesday or Wednesday."

Anna looked over to Mike and Kate. "Where will we go? Where will we live when Oliver gets released?"

Mike answered. "Until we get to the bottom of this story, you will stay put and we will find a separate safe house for Oliver. Then, it will be witness protection for both of you."

"Why can't we be together?" Oliver demanded to know.

"You know that would put you both in more danger," Kate said softly. "We can protect you better when you're apart. We've bent the rules a little too far just letting Anna come see you."

Oliver nodded. He understood but he didn't like it.

He smiled at his sister. "How did you convince them to let you come here? They told me they had you hidden away."

Anna looked at Mike and Kate, and she suddenly felt very nervous.

Oliver noticed her silence. "Anna, what is it you're not telling me?" he asked tensely.

She picked his phone up off the nightstand and asked him to open it. Once he did, she went to his mailbox, and as she suspected, he had an email from the genealogy company. She opened it and handed it to him to read. Everyone in the room was silent, waiting for Oliver's reaction.

It took a few minutes for him to absorb what he'd read. He looked at Anna in disbelief, shaking his head slowly. "This is impossible. I remember Mom and Dad fighting over adopting you. She'd never have adopted Dad's illegitimate child."

"But she did, and we'll never know why."

Oliver was furious. He threw his phone at the end of the bed; it struck the footboard. "No! You're my adopted sister. You're not the daughter of one of my father's whores! This is wrong. We are NOT blood relatives. Do you hear me?"

Anna recoiled from her brother's rage. She backed toward the door just as the nurse rushed in.

"What's going on here? He's in tachycardia! I told you people not to upset him. Get out, now." She looked specifically at a horrified Anna.

The nurse inserted a syringe into Oliver's IV. "Okay, deep breaths. Your heart is going to slow down very quickly with the propranolol I just gave you." She gave a nasty look to the agents.

Anna had already fled the room and was leaning against the elevator bank.

Kate tried to comfort her, but Anna pushed her off. "Just get me out of here, now!"

Anna remained silent all the way back to the field office. She couldn't even cry. She had nothing left inside of her.

***

"Get in here," Harland yelled down the hall at Mike, Kate and Anna. He opened the door to an empty interview room and ushered them in. "Where the hell have you been?"

Mike waved away the question. "It doesn't matter right now. We need to get Anna to the house."

Harland looked at Mike and then at the distraught young woman, barely able to stand.

He opened the door. "Let's go, Ms. Cahill. Your escort is here to take you back."

Mike and Kate tried to go with her, but Harland held them back.

"We still need to have a discussion about your field trip."

Anna looked at them with empty eyes. "Who do I trust now?" she asked, not expecting an answer.

Two new agents, one in front and one behind her, walked her down the hallway to the waiting car.

CHAPTER 25

February 24, 2017

Anna was at her kitchen table, working on a PowerPoint presentation for one of her midterms when her doorbell rang. She sighed and closed her laptop. This would be the third time this week her neighbor Maya needed to borrow something. She opened her door, ready to tease her absent-minded friend, when she stepped back in surprise.

"Hello, my beautiful love!" Jay was standing in the doorway with a bouquet of two dozen multicolored roses.

Anna screamed in excitement, pulled him inside and gave him a fervent kiss.

"These are gorgeous! What are you doing here? We spoke last night. You didn't tell me you were coming!"

"That would have ruined the surprise." Jay smiled widely. "This isn't inconvenient for you, is it?" He suddenly felt trepidation at dropping in on his newly-minted significant other.

"Never! I'm so happy you're here." Anna put the flowers on the table and started to lead him into the bedroom.

He hesitated. "I need to take a shower. I had a couple of meetings this morning and then went right to O'Hare to catch a flight."

"Perfect." Anna continued to pull him into her room. "We can take one together."

Jay smiled. He was sure there'd be no hot water left in the whole building by the time their shower was over.

***

They were lounging on the sofa when Anna announced she was hungry. She was sporting a sweatshirt and leggings, while Jay was dressed in flannel pajama pants and a long-sleeved T-shirt.

He hugged her close to him. "I'm starving but I feel too lazy to get dressed," he lamented.

"No worries, we have a great Asian place here that delivers. Let me get the menu for you."

Anna hopped up and grabbed the menu out of the kitchen drawer. She took a moment to smell her roses, now in a vase on the counter. While Jay read the menu items, Anna put her legs in his lap and snuggled into his shoulder.

"I can't believe you couldn't go ten days without seeing me," she joked.

"You're addictive." Jay punctuated his statement with a kiss. "Okay, let's order. Get me whatever you're having and add an order of spring rolls."

While Anna placed the order, Jay popped into the bedroom. When she hung up, she noticed he had come back with a small box for her to open.

He couldn't miss the shock on her face. "It's not *that*, but it is something to show my commitment to you."

Anna opened the box. Inside was a brilliant princess-cut sapphire surrounded by diamonds, set in white gold. Her gasp was audible.

Jay slipped the ring on her right-hand ring finger. "Sapphire is your birthstone, isn't it?"

Anna was so breathless she could only nod.

"It's a promise ring," he explained. "Whenever you're ready, I will buy you an engagement ring that will put that" —he pointed at the two-carat, velvety blue ring— "to shame."

"Jay, you know the cost of the ring doesn't matter to me. It's the commitment that means everything."

Jay pulled her into his lap and kissed her ardently. "I never want you to doubt how much I love you. I'll never leave you, and I'll always protect you."

"I love you so much." Anna put her arms around his neck and melted into him.

She could have stayed that way all night, but the food delivery was prompt, eliciting a laugh from Jay.

"What do you love more? Your sweet and sour shrimp or me?" he said.

"Both," Anna giggled as she laid out plates and served up dinner.

They spent the rest of the weekend soaking each other in, never leaving the apartment.

When it was time for Jay to leave on Monday, Anna cried.

He tried to comfort her. "I need to go to Dubai one last time."

"How long will you be gone?" she asked through her tears.

"Just long enough to pack some things and get ready for my permanent move to Chicago. Maybe a week? Besides, you have your spring break trip to Aruba with your girlfriends. I should be the one crying. Just thinking of you on a beach in your bikini with other guys around makes me jealous."

"You shouldn't be. You're the only man I want." Anna reassured him with a kiss.

Jay wiped away her tears.

"Call me as soon as you get home," she reminded him as he went out to meet his taxi.

She felt dejected as she dressed for her afternoon lecture. On her way to the parking garage, she ran into the mail carrier.

She waved to him. "Hi, Sam."

"Miss Cahill, hold on. I have some mail for you."

She thanked him and continued to her car to get the heat running. While the warmth seeped through the car, still in the garage, she flipped through bills and advertisements.

There it was: a pristine, white envelope with the Northwestern logo.

CHAPTER 26

March 14, 2017

Anna stood at the counter in the Naperville house, picking at microwave mac and cheese. The previous day had been spent holed up in her room, searching for adoption records with no luck. She'd finally texted Kate DeSoto and asked for help. Kate had been compassionate throughout this ordeal, and that made her Anna's go-to. The agent had texted her that morning that she'd stop by that afternoon.

After giving up on trying to eat, Anna joined the two agents assigned to protect her in the great room. Today was the first day of the NCAA basketball tournament, and they had high hopes for Northwestern. She soon tired of the game and took her laptop to the office to see if her midterm grades had been posted.

Why am I even looking? It's not like I can graduate from OSU when I'm hidden away in witness protection. Anna laid her head on the desk, deflated.

A knock on the office door made her jump.

"Sorry! I didn't mean to startle you. Is everything ok?" Kate asked.

"I started checking my midterm grades and realized it's pointless. I'm never going to get to graduate. Anna Cahill isn't going to exist anymore. Law school is out of the picture, too."

Kate took a seat in the chair opposite. "You may not get your degree as Anna Cahill, but you have earned it. Under your new identity, we can ask the witness protection team to get you a diploma, just not from OSU."

Anna sighed. She had typed up a list of questions yesterday in her obnoxious amount of spare time. She opened the document on her computer and readied a pad and paper.

"Are you interviewing me?" Kate asked jokingly.

"Sort of. I have a bunch of questions, so I wrote them down. I'm hoping you can answer them or find out the answers for me."

Kate was a bit uncomfortable. She sympathized with the young woman's situation and grief, but she was an agent first and couldn't disclose a whole lot. She had already gone into a gray area looking for adoption information for her. "I'll do my best, but I can't make any promises."

Anna could feel her face getting blotchy with frustration, but she nodded her understanding.

"First, do I need to identify the bodies of my family members? The shooting was four days ago."

"Your Uncle David's ex-wife already did the identification on him and your parents. Don't worry about that."

"What about funeral arrangements? Will I be allowed to attend?"

Kate hesitated for a moment. "Anna, Oliver is the executor of your parents' will and he is going to be the one to make arrangements. He'll be released from the hospital tomorrow, so I imagine he's going to speak to my supervisor about how to handle the burial. You can't attend as you are the only witness in an ongoing homicide investigation. I'm not sure if Oliver can even be there, since he is the only survivor."

The memory of Oliver's anger and emphatic denial that they were blood relatives was still fresh in her mind, and Anna bit her lip at the idea she would be completely shut out of everything. She didn't care about her father, but her heart wouldn't accept that her mother hadn't loved her. Maybe in the beginning Anna's adoption was to torment Thomas, but she didn't think Meredith could fake affection for twenty-two years.

"When will I enter witness protection? Who will know I'm there? I don't trust anyone in the FBI outside of you and SA Mallory."

"The witness protection program runs separately from the FBI. All I know is your case is in process. Tremendous work goes into putting someone in permanent protection. You are right to be careful about who you trust. Remember that, even once you are in your new location."

"Last question—but I withhold my right to ask more at a further date." Anna stopped when she noticed Kate smiling. "What?"

"You sound like a lawyer already. We aren't in a courtroom, Anna. I will try to tell you the truth as much as I'm allowed in my capacity with the FBI."

"Fair enough."

Kate knew the next question before Anna asked. She had been having a conversation with herself all morning about how to handle the situation.

"Did you find anything about my biological mother?" Anna's voice trembled as she asked.

"Are you sure you really want to know? It's not what you might've expected."

Anna nodded her head. "Whatever it is, I need to know."

"Your mother was twenty when she had you. She was an exchange student from a university in Sweden. She had blonde hair and blue eyes. Shortly after giving birth to you, she developed an amniotic fluid embolism. She died a few hours after you were born."

Devastation rushed through Anna. She felt gutted. "That's why Meredith adopted me. I was Thomas' child and my birth mother was dead. She never held it against me." Tears pricked her eyes.

"Perhaps that's why she always reminded you that you were adopted. She wanted to be sure you didn't know Thomas was your father," Kate surmised.

"Do you know what her name was?" Anna asked quietly.

"Yes. Thea Henricksson."

"Can you find out her family's address in Sweden?"

"Even if I had that ability, which I don't, I couldn't share that information with you. As it is, I've used my FBI access inappropriately. This could get me fired," Kate stressed.

Anger seeped into every pore of Anna's body. With a sweep of her arm, she knocked her laptop off the desk and sent it crashing to the floor. She stood up and slammed her open hands against the wall.

"Everything in my life is a lie! It's never going to change. Someone is making a new identity for me right now and I'll have to live that lie until the day I die!"

"Anna, calm down. You've learned her identity. That's something." Kate tried to sound encouraging.

Anna plopped back in her chair. "Yeah, and I also know my dad slept with a girl younger than me and got her pregnant. She could have been nineteen at the time. It disgusts me that he is my biological father!" She put her hands over her face in defeat.

Kate noticed the large sapphire and diamond ring on her right hand. "That's new." She pointed to Anna's finger. "Where did that come from?"

"Jay gave it to me last month, as a sign of his commitment to me."

"I didn't notice you wearing it before. Why do you have it on now?" It was Kate's turn to ask the questions.

"I had it packed in my bag. Oliver didn't like the fact I was dating Jay. If he'd noticed it, my surprise news about law school would have been overshadowed by a fight over who I was dating. I remembered it was in my suitcase yesterday, so I put it back on. I couldn't care less what Oliver thinks anymore. Besides, Jay didn't do this or else he wouldn't have received immunity."

"Anna." Kate leaned forward. "Don't mention Jay's immunity to anyone. You shouldn't know about it. Jay's life would be in danger if anyone finds out."

"What, why?" She was panicking.

"Just don't, ok? Unless it's a mundane request, direct all your communication to either me or Mike Mallory."

Kate's tone silenced Anna. She hadn't wanted to believe that she and Jay were still in such danger.

"I know you have more questions. If you're worried about your things at your house and apartment, it'll all be taken care of by the relocation team. Someone should reach out to you from witness protection very soon. As far as the family business, all assets are frozen due to our ongoing investigation."

"I don't give a damn about the Cahill family business or their money!"

Kate resigned herself to Anna's discontent. "I need to get going. Text me if something comes up and I'll get back to you as quick as I can." She stood and exited the office, scolded the agents watching the basketball game for not staying alert and retreated to her car.

Kate was grateful for the forty-minute drive back to the office. She turned the volume up on her favorite nineties music station and sang as loud as she could to decompress.

CHAPTER 27

March 14, 2017

Jay was getting anxious with so many people crowded into his hotel suite, his leg unconsciously shaking while he sat on the couch. Kirkland, Harland, Mike and Ballenger were all standing in a circle, talking. Jay looked at his watch. It was nine o'clock in the morning.

"Mr. Mizra, we're ready to begin." Ballenger summoned him to the dining room, where they all took their seats. Jay put his cell phone down on the table.

Kirkland began his instructions for the fifth time since yesterday morning. "You'll call your father on speaker so we can record the conversation and hear what you are saying. Keep it in English. If you or your father speak in Arabic, our translator back at the office will let us know everything you said."

"What if my father isn't forthcoming with the name of his supplier? Or he doesn't admit to the Cahill murders? What then?"

Mike could smell Mizra's nerves from the far end of the table. "Let him know about the murders. We can gauge his response by his reaction. Ask him the name of his source. If he questions you, tell him you want to meet him in person to discuss setting the shipment up. Calm the supplier's nerves, so to speak. Got it?"

Jay nodded and wiped the sweat from his forehead.

"If at any time you think he suspects something, disconnect the call. You can tell him later it dropped."

Harland was eyeing Mizra. "Maybe we should hold off another thirty minutes or so. Get Jahir some coffee, let him settle his nerves."

"No!" Jay looked at his watch. It was already nine-fifteen. "It's after six in the evening in Dubai. At sundown my father will have Maghrib; it is the fourth call to prayer of the day and always at sundown. I must call him before that."

"Then get on the phone," Kirkland demanded.

Jay set the phone to speaker mode. With shaking hands, he dialed the number and placed it on a folded towel in the middle of the table. The towel would muffle the echo so his father wouldn't realize he was on speaker.

The phone picked up.

"Baba? It's Jahir."

"Jahir, what have you found out? Parishad and I have been waiting patiently."

Jay mouthed "brother-in-law" to Harland, who was sitting across from him. "Baba, I'm sorry for the delay. The Cahill family has been murdered. My driver, Aalam, was found dead at the scene. The FBI suspect him of the killings."

"Good! Let the blame fall on him. What about the FBI? Are they still following you?"

"They questioned me after the murders. I told them I had no knowledge. They ruled me out when they found Barakat's body."

"Excellent! We are running out of time."

"Baba, give me the name of your supplier and FBI contact. I can set up a meeting with the three of us so the FBI agent can confirm the investigation is over."

Harland was writing furiously on a notepad and stuck it in front of Jay.

Tell him to wire you the money for the guns and you will bring it to the supplier as a show of faith.

"Wire the money to me. I will bring it to your supplier as a show of faith."

"I will text you the names and phone numbers. If they agree to the meeting, then I will send you the money. Demonstrate your worth, Jahir. Do not bring shame on your family."

"Baba, I won't fail you. I'll call as soon as the meeting is set." Jay looked at Ballenger, who nodded encouragingly to him.

Hadiq ibn Khalid al-Mizra disconnected the line.

The room was silent until the text chime on Jay's phone. He tried to pick it up, but Kirkland grabbed it first.

"Lieutenant Colonel James Benson. Son of a bitch! This is a Georgia area code. This guy's at Fort Stewart!"

Ballenger asked the obvious question. "What is so important about Fort Stewart?"

"It just so happens to be the largest Army installation east of the Mississippi River. It represents the US Army's world-class training and military armored power projection on the Eastern Seaboard."

Harland interrupted Kirkland's tirade. "Who is the mole in the FBI?"

Kirkland looked back at the phone and then at Harland and Mike. "It's Brian Nelson."

"Shit!" Mike jumped up and pulled out his phone.

"What's going on?" Kirkland asked in surprise.

"Brian Nelson has been guarding Oliver Cahill at the hospital. I've got to get him picked up right now!"

"Make sure you sequester him. You know where to take him." Harland put his coat back on and hustled out of the suite.

Mike's call was answered on the second ring. "Garrett?" he asked. "Where are you right now?"

"I'm leaving the office to head to the hospital to check in on Cahill."

"I'll meet you there in fifteen minutes. Don't let Nelson enter Oliver's room. Don't spook him either. I'll call you from the car and explain." Mike took off running.

Kirkland forwarded Hadiq's text to his phone and gave Jay back his. "Good job, Jahir. Stay here and talk to no one. We'll let you know to set up the meet after we interrogate Nelson."

"What if he doesn't cooperate?" Jay asked.

Kirkland let out a wicked laugh and sauntered out the door.

Jay looked at Ballenger, the only other person remaining in the room.

"He's right," he said. "You did well. That was tremendous pressure. Make sure you don't talk to anyone about this and don't try to contact Anna. She's off-limits."

Jay threw his phone back on the table and went to sit on the sofa, groaning in frustration. "I'm innocent but I'm still trapped!"

Ballenger looked around the large suite. "It beats the hell out of an FBI holding cell. Remember, talk to no one without me present. Put me on speed dial." He picked Jay's phone up off the table and threw it to him. Jay caught it as Ballenger made his exit.

CHAPTER 28

March 15, 2017

Harland pulled inside the warehouse, and the doors closed behind him. Mike, Garrett and McCormack were waiting as he stepped out of his car. Mike had gathered the only agents he knew could be trusted in the entire Chicago field office, apart from his partner. Kate had wanted to come to the black site, but Mike refused. Kate had a brief romantic history with Brian Nelson from when she first transferred to Chicago. She'd filled Mike in last night when he called to bring her up to speed. Nelson couldn't handle that Kate had been promoted to senior special agent when he was not. His jealousy ended their brief affair.

SA Brian Nelson had been strapped to a chair inside a caged area since yesterday afternoon. Temperatures were below freezing; the emptiness of the warehouse didn't provide any warmth.

As Harland joined the agents around the portable heater, Mike filled him in on their lack of progress.

"No luck. We've been taking shifts for the past twenty-four hours with him, but the only thing out of this asshole's mouth is expletives."

"Have you called Rudy yet?" Harland asked.

McCormack jumped in. "Yup, he should be here any minute. He hasn't failed to extract a confession yet."

Harland nodded his approval. "Let's hope he keeps his record. I hate to leave you boys in the cold but its best I not be here when Rudy interrogates Nelson."

"We're good," Mike assured him. "Go ahead. We'll keep you posted."

Harland popped his trunk and grabbed a blanket. "Here, give him this so he doesn't get hypothermia. He won't be any use to us then."

Garrett opened the cage door and threw the blanket around the shivering Nelson.

Harland got back in his car and exited through the now open doors. As he exited the alley, he passed Rudy. Neither man acknowledged the other.

Nelson recognized Rudy the moment he entered the warehouse.

"No! You are violating my rights. I want my lawyer here now."

Mike could see Nelson's breath as it came in short bursts out of his mouth.

"Why don't you tell us about how you provided confidential information to a military officer? Or why you didn't report the illegal sale of US weapons to a terrorist group?" Mike grinned nastily.

"Fuck you!" Nelson yelled, his voice cracking from lack of water and the cold.

Mike shrugged as he pulled the cage door wide open. "Your choice."

Mike walked away as Rudy entered with his tool bag. With the other agents, he headed to the heated office on the other side of the warehouse.

"McCormack, you've been here since midnight. Why don't you go home and get some rest?" he suggested.

"And miss this dirtbag getting what he deserves? Not a chance. I'll hang out a while longer."

McCormack was old-school. He was in special forces before he joined the FBI; torturing a traitor didn't bother him.

It took thirty minutes, four detached fingernails and a wound to the side of the head by a blunt object for Nelson to give up the information. Mike again entered the cage, this time with an extra chair and an audio recorder.

"Let's hear it, and I mean everything. Rudy has no other plans today."

Rudy smiled and nodded at Nelson.

"Alright! Benson contacted me and asked if I'd keep my eyes open for any investigations regarding arms dealing. He offered me two hundred and fifty thousand dollars if I gave him a heads up." Nelson's face was covered in sweat despite the cold. Neither Mike nor Rudy did anything to stem the bleeding from his forehead and fingers.

"How did the Lieutenant Colonel come to contact you? Why did he think you would be willing to turn on your government for a piss amount of cash?" Mike's anger made his voice rise.

"My stepbrother is his son-in-law. When I applied to the Bureau, Benson wrote a letter of recommendation for me. I owed him."

"You owed him treason for a letter recommending you as an FBI agent? A bit of a paradox, wouldn't you say? I think there is more to the story."

When Nelson shook his head, Mike nodded to Rudy. He reached into his bag and pulled out a vise-grip.

"Start with the molars," Mike directed.

"Wait!" Nelson pleaded.

"Oh, do you have something else to share? If it's not the whole truth this time, Rudy is going to remove every tooth in your jackass head."

"We were drinking pretty heavy…" Nelson paused and eyed Rudy before turning back to Mike. "I vented hard to my stepbrother about no promotions after eighteen years on the job. I told him I had zero loyalty to the Bureau, I was just waiting out my retirement. He must have mentioned it to Benson. Two weeks later, the Lieutenant Colonel paid me a visit. When I got wind you and DeSoto were investigating a foreign national with a potential military source for arms dealing, I reached out to him."

"You're a disgrace to your country." Mike wanted to put this guy in the ground, but they still needed him to contact the lieutenant colonel.

"Who has his phone?" he asked the other two agents standing in the office doorway.

"I do." McCormack brought the phone out and handed it to Mike.

Garrett followed on his heels. They all wanted to listen in on Nelson's call to Benson.

"Now, call him and tell him the investigation is closed and the foreign national was released with an apology from the FBI. If he asks why, say they found the assassin who killed the Cahill family dead at the scene. The murders had nothing to do with arms dealings. Case closed."

"I need my hands free to call," Nelson pleaded.

Garrett glared at him. "I'll hold the phone for you. It'll be on speaker so we all can listen in."

McCormack pulled out his gun and held it to Nelson's head. "Just in case you decide to warn him." He smiled maliciously.

While the three agents listened to Brian Nelson's very convincing phone call, Rudy took a roll of plastic out of his SUV and laid it on the floor of the warehouse. Once the call was done, Mike took the SIM card out of the phone and tucked it in Nelson's pocket. The agents started walking to their cars.

"Wait! I did what you wanted. Aren't you going to cut me loose? I need medical attention."

"Don't worry," Mike said without turning around. "Rudy will take care of all that."

As Mike closed the warehouse behind him, he heard a muffled "pop". He got in his car and drove home in time for his wife's homemade meatloaf dinner.

CHAPTER 29

March 17, 2017

Oliver stared at the clock on the paneled wall of the conference room. He mentally counted down the minutes until the moment when, a week ago today, he would have been shot. Grateful to be alive, he still felt pain in his leg, and crutches leaned against the wall behind him. Despite his gratitude, he felt an underlying irritation. The doctor had told him he would feel withdrawal effects from the heavy sedation he'd had while hospitalized; upon discharge, the strength of his pain medication had been reduced and the quantity was limited.

Oliver believed this was more than withdrawal. His displeasure was directed toward Anna. And toward his deceased father for allowing one of his bastards into their family.

Jack Harland sat at the end of the table, to Oliver's left. Harvey Latimer, Oliver's parents' attorney, sat across from him. Once Anna arrived, Mr. Latimer would read his parents' will. Oliver could tell the lawyer felt awed by his surroundings. Not many will readings took place at the FBI offices, but Harland had insisted it was the safest place.

Mike arrived with Anna shortly after one o'clock. She went to sit beside Oliver, but he pushed the chair in, winning a nasty look from Mike as he helped Anna into the seat at the end of the table.

Mike pulled out the chair next to Oliver and sat down. Oliver didn't like the agent sitting next to him; he felt his anger might boil over at any time and knew that Mike, despite his age, could take him down in a minute.

"Before the reading begins, I want to make it clear all funds related to Cahill Investment Bankers are frozen, pending our ongoing investigation. As the residences, cars, jewelry and investments left by your parents were likely bought with ill-gotten gains, there is also a freeze on selling any of them. Cash money will be held in escrow until a resolution has been reached." Harland finished his speech and motioned to Mr. Latimer to begin.

"What is the point of even having a will reading if there is nothing to be received?" Oliver spat.

"You better watch your tone, young man, and remember why you're here in the first place," Harland said.

Oliver understood the reference to his immunity agreement. He bit his tongue.

Mr. Latimer cleared his throat and began. "This is the last will and testament of Thomas Paul Cahill and Meredith Watters Cahill." He paused for a moment. "Before we begin, I should preface the reading by stating this will is dated and signed the fourth of February 1993. Your parents intended to change it after Anna's adoption, but it was never finalized."

Oliver grinned and looked at Anna. Her expression never changed, nor did she remove her eyes from the table in front of her.

Latimer continued with the reading, though it was unnecessary. After Tommy's death in October 1992, his parents had changed their will and left everything to their only heir, Oliver. Anna was not to receive even a trinket.

Latimer put the will back in its folder and handed it to Oliver. Oliver stood up gingerly, balancing the folder and grabbing his crutches. Mike had pushed his chair out, blocking Oliver's path, while he went to stand behind a somber Anna. Harland led Latimer out of the conference room and back to the main entrance.

Oliver started walking around the other side of the table, but Mike closed the door before he could reach it.

"Why don't you have a seat for a moment, Oliver? Anna has a few questions she needs to ask you." The question was rhetorical.

Oliver sat down in the chair recently occupied by Harland, his crutches balanced against his leg.

"What the hell do you want?" Every word out of his mouth was laced with ire.

"I found out some information about my birth mother," Anna said. "I thought you might be able to provide additional details."

"What information? It was a closed adoption. Besides, I was only seven years old."

"My mother was twenty years old when she gave birth to me. She had blonde hair, blue eyes and was an exchange student from a university in Sweden. She passed away a few hours after I was born. She might have been an intern at Cahill Investments. Could you ask some of the older employees if they remember her? Her name was Thea Henricksson." Anna looked at Oliver for the first time since she entered the room.

Oliver's face turned red with fury. He started cursing as he attempted to stand and steady himself on his crutches.

Anna stood up to stop him. "Why can't you help me? It's not my fault what our father did. I didn't adopt myself into the family!"

Oliver visibly struggled with his emotions. There was a part of him that wanted to embrace his sister, acknowledge none of this was her fault. Anger won out. "Your mother was my fucking nanny! She slept at our house every night. I cared about her and one day she was gone. No explanation. Now I know why. She was a money-grubbing whore who took advantage of my father's grief. I'm glad my parents never changed their will. You deserve nothing, just like your mother!" he screamed so loud that people in the hallway turned to look through the windows at the front of the conference room.

"Oliver, please," she implored. "Can you tell me anything about her, like her hometown? After today you won't ever have to see me again."

"Fuck you and your mother!" Oliver gritted his teeth. He stumbled to the door and opened it. SA Garrett was waiting outside to take him back to his new residence.

Oliver felt nothing but rage as he followed behind the special agent. Logically, he knew Anna wasn't to blame but right now, he came first. His physical and emotional pain were overwhelming. All his anger on was focused on Anna.

**

Anna sat back down and put her head on the table. Mike didn't know how to comfort her, so he texted Kate, who was at her desk. She soon appeared and nodded for him to leave the room. He did so with relief.

Feelings of devastation and resentment overwhelmed Anna. She appreciated Kate's presence, but she was beyond comfort.

"She was the nanny." Anna looked up in disbelief. "My mother didn't seduce Thomas. More than likely, he forced himself on her or took advantage of his position."

"Anna, give yourself time to process all this, ok?"

"I know he knows something, but he'll never tell me. He despises me for something I had no control over. How can he go from loving me to hating me in an instant?"

"You both have been through a series of traumatic events. Everyone copes differently. He will eventually come around." Kate tried to soothe her.

"I won't be here though, will I? You said yourself that I'll be gone in another week. He won't be able to find me, and I won't be able to find him."

"One thing at a time." Kate slowly coaxed Anna out of her chair. "I'm going to take you back so you can rest." She wanted to bypass a panic attack if possible.

Anna nodded and followed Kate to her car. She no longer felt guilty over the fifteen million dollars Meredith had left her. It bothered her, however, that Oliver was behaving exactly like she had predicted. He was the only family she had left, and he'd just slammed the door in her face and bolted it shut.

CHAPTER 30

March 18, 2017

The gathering in Jay Mizra's suite was smaller this morning, but that didn't lower the tension. Harland, Kirkland and Ballenger sat around the dining table again, the towel back in the center to muffle the echo from the speakerphone. Jay was pacing back and forth in front of the picture window, oblivious to the view.

"Jay, it's time."

He nodded and took his seat at the table.

Harland continued, "Tell him you have his money and want to meet for the exchange. Most likely, he will want you to fly to Savannah. Be agreeable. If he wants to meet earlier than Wednesday, tell him you can't get a private plane before then. He won't expect you to fly commercial." He turned on the recorder.

Jay took a sip of water, put the phone on speaker and called Lieutenant Colonel Benson.

He answered on the third ring. "Benson."

"This is Jay al-Mizra, Lieutenant Colonel," Jay began, using the Arabic form of his last name.

"Don't use my rank! Tell me if you've got it."

"Yes. I have the required amount and am ready to deliver to you. The recipient of your deliverables is getting anxious. I hope you're ready to make an immediate delivery."

"Of course I am! We'll meet on Monday. I'll text you the address."

Jay looked panicked. Harland lowered his hand, reminding him to stay calm.

"I can't get a private plane until Wednesday. We can meet on the tarmac at the executive airport in Savannah. I'll text you the tail number of the plane and my arrival time on Wednesday morning. Agreed?"

They could hear Benson take a deep breath. "Will you be bringing a friend?"

Jay looked at Harland, confused. Harland quickly wrote SA Nelson on a notepad and shook his head.

"I don't trust anyone else. It will just be me. I expect it to be just you. No one else." Jay surprised himself with how stern he sounded.

Benson went for it. "Alright. I'll expect your text on Wednesday morning."

The phone went silent.

Kirkland sat back in his chair. "Excellent! Now let's call your father and get him to wire the money. Do you know how much it will be?"

Jay shook his head. "I have no idea. I need to reserve a plane." He was stressing, thinking of everything that could go wrong.

"Leave that to us," Harland said. "We'll arrange a private plane, and you will have backup onsite in Savannah. Now, let's get that wire ready for Monday."

A little more water and Jay was on the phone with his father. It was five-thirty in the evening in Dubai.

"Baba?" Jay emulated Harland, keeping his voice calm and steady.

"Jahir! Tell me you have news for me." Everyone at the table could hear the anxiety in Hadiq ibn Khalid al-Mizra's voice.

"I'm meeting the supplier Wednesday. I need to have the funds ready before then. Can you transfer it to my account?"

"No wires. I have contacts in Chicago that will get the cash to you. When we hang up, text me the hotel address and room number. They will deliver to you on Monday. Be in your room."

Jay saw Kirkland and Harland stiffen. They didn't like the delivery system. He raised his hands, silently questioning them.

Harland quickly wrote: *Two delivery men and you need to know how much cash to expect.*

"Baba, I don't know these people. No more than two colleagues making the delivery, ok? How much are they bringing me?"

"Only two will come. Why do you need to know how much money?" Hadiq sounded suspicious.

"How else am I supposed to know if I have the correct amount? What if the supplier asks me for more than I have? I won't know if he's cheating me, and I'll likely be killed."

There was silence on the line, so Jay took a chance. "Baba, if you don't trust your only son, send one of your men to make the delivery," he said with as much irritation as he could muster.

It worked.

"Forgive me, Jahir. You're doing as I asked. It's difficult not to be paranoid. You will be delivering five million dollars. Our supplier knows he'll get the other half once Hamas has received the shipment."

"I'll text you my hotel information now and text again after the money is delivered to the supplier. I presume you will know once the guns reach their destination?"

"Yes. Don't worry about that. You are serving us well, Jahir. I'll wait to hear of your victory Wednesday." Jay's father disconnected.

Jay picked up the phone and texted him his address.

The tension in the room turned to repressed excitement. Harland and Kirkland had been waiting nearly a year to catch the traitor. Jay, though, was worried what would happen to him when his father found out it was a set-up.

Ballenger read his mind. "How are you going to protect Jay once you arrest Benson? It won't take long for it to get back to his father and brother-in-law. You heard Hadiq say he has people in Chicago already. There will be a target on my client's back."

This was Kirkland's purview. "We can arrest you when we arrest Benson and make it appear you are caught up in the sting," he told Jay. "Blame will likely fall on SA Nelson for providing Benson with false information. If you provide an affidavit about your father and brother-in-law's involvement in arming Hamas, we can put you in our witness protection program."

Jay immediately saw a hole in the strategy. "If I'm arrested, my father will have me assassinated so I can't link the sale back to him. If I provide an affidavit, there is no guarantee the UAE, Dubai specifically, would extradite my family members to the United States to stand trial."

"What do you suggest then?" Harland was frustrated.

"Arrest me but release me as soon as Benson drives away. Give me a new set of documents under a new name, and I will disappear on my own." Jay looked to Ballenger to see his reaction.

He nodded his agreement. "My client is correct. He risks his life either way. If you have a better plan, let's hear it. I seriously doubt, however, you can make Jay invisible through witness protection."

Harland took a moment to process the different scenarios in his head. He looked at Jay and Ballenger. "You give us a signed affidavit about your father and brother-in-law's involvement in the illegal purchase of guns, and we will provide you with a new identity and documents. Then you will be on your own. We won't place you in the program."

Jay was leery, but Ballenger gave him a nod. This was the best deal he'd get, and he needed a new identity. "Fine, I'll do it."

"From this moment on, you talk to no one but the three men seated at this table. Mike Mallory will be here on Monday as backup when your delivery comes. Don't worry, he'll stay well hidden. This suite is bigger than my house," Harland quipped.

"I'll type up an affidavit for Mr. Mizra," Ballenger said. "He will sign it once he has been 'released' from custody and given new documents."

Within moments, Jay was again alone in his hotel room. He went to the side table in the master bedroom and took his private phone from the drawer. How could he be expected not to talk to her? He sighed and placed the phone back on the table.

CHAPTER 31

March 20, 2017

Anna paced back and forth in her bedroom. She couldn't accept Oliver cutting her off so harshly. He had always looked after her. Her heart felt as if it would shatter if they couldn't resolve this before she was taken to her new location.

She picked up her cell phone and called him.

He let it ring four times before picking it up. "I don't know what you want from me, Anna." His words were terse.

"I want my brother back. Oliver, you must see this isn't my fault. Punishing me for something our dad did isn't going to solve anything."

"That doesn't mean I'm ready to accept that we have the same father."

Anna could feel the anger building in her chest, but she didn't want Oliver to block her number. "In another week, I'll be out of your life forever," she reasoned. "Is this how you want our relationship to end? You're my big brother. We are the only family we have left."

Oliver knew he should be apologetic, but instead he was annoyed. "I can't deal with this right now, Anna. Deep down, I did love you but if I'm honest, I'm happy that you are about to disappear from my life."

"You're going to regret this one day." Anna held back her tears.

She heard a dial tone.

Within an hour, Kate DeSoto was knocking on her door.

Surprised, Anna opened it. "Is everything okay?"

"No. Oliver called SA Mallory and told him you reached out. I've been sent to confiscate your cell phone. I should have done it a long time ago."

"What? My friends are just getting back from spring break and are going to hear on the news my family was murdered. They'll try to reach me, especially if I'm not at my apartment. I need to let them know I'm ok and what is going to happen to me." Anna was infuriated.

"Exactly why I need your phone. No one can know that you are going into the WITSEC program. That's what it's called: Witness Security Program. You should know because that's how the US Marshal handling your immersion will refer to it."

"It's exile. Do the semantics really matter?" Anna huffed as she handed Kate her phone. "There, now all my friends can think I'm either kidnapped or dead somewhere. They're all I have left. You told me to text you or SA Mallory if I needed something. I'm not supposed to trust anyone else. How can I do that if you take my phone?"

Kate wanted to be sympathetic but she had already been chewed out by Harland for the hospital trip. One more screw up and she would be riding a desk in Peoria. "Anna, I understand you're frustrated. None of this was of your doing but you're being affected by it just the same. Please realize we're trying to protect you. SA McCormack and SA Garrett are being assigned to watch you on alternating shifts, along with a second agent from now until the US Marshal comes. You can trust either of them."

Kate stood up.

"Wait, please. When is the US Marshal coming for me?"

"He's expected to be here on Thursday." Kate walked out the door.

Anna began to panic. Jay would help her, surely. Oliver had shut her down, but she still had Jay. Hadn't he just professed his love for her? She needed to reach him.

***

Anna waited an hour and then descended the stairs. The two agents on duty were right where she expected them to be, in front of the TV, watching the NCAA basketball tournament. She sat on the sofa beside Agent McCormack.

"Hey, Anna," he said. "Do you need something or are you interested in the game?"

"I need something," Anna whispered so he had to lean in to hear her. "I need to go to the drugstore."

"This house is stocked. There can't be anything you possibly need at the drugstore. If it's a prescription, I can have Garrett pick it up on his way in tonight."

"I need to buy tampons."

Anna kept her face expressionless. McCormack, a war-hardened ex-soldier, shifted uncomfortably.

"Oh. We never thought of that."

"Do you want me to write down exactly what brand and size I need? It's kind of an emergency." Anna smiled awkwardly.

McCormack cleared his throat. "I think a quick run over to the drugstore will be okay."

"Great! Let me get my purse."

When they reached the store, McCormack positioned himself at the front door while Anna quickly made her way to the correct aisle and grabbed two boxes. Looking at the door, she could see McCormack had his back to her. She quickly went down another aisle and grabbed a couple of burner phones. She paid in cash at the pharmacy and requested a paper bag for her purchases. She knew the agents would never look inside.

Once they were back at the house, she took the bag upstairs. She didn't know where Jay was but decided to wait until she went to bed to text him, just in case he had agents around him.

CHAPTER 32

March 24, 2017

Oliver approved of his new surroundings. The safe house was in Barrington on a residential street with beautiful, brick, upper-middle-class homes. It had a first-floor master bedroom, which suited him fine. He could walk without crutches, but he was still in pain.

Voices in the foyer signaled the arrival of Kirkland and Harland. The time had come for Oliver's part in this fiasco to be wrapped up.

He followed the voices to the dining room and joined the two men at the table.

"How are you feeling?" Kirkland asked politely.

"It hurts like a son of a bitch, but at least I'm off the crutches."

Oliver's agitation did not go unnoticed. Harland addressed what he assumed had Oliver in such a foul mood. "I know you are anxious about the estate left by your parents. The business is officially closed. Our forensic accountants are going through the books for Cahill Investment Bankers and your parents' bank account records. Unless you can provide a list of which employees were involved in the OFAC blacklist accounts, we won't be able to offer severance to any of your former employees."

Oliver just shook his head. He knew he could provide a few names but had no idea how many had been involved over the years.

"What about my family home?" he said. "It should be worth close to three million dollars, and it was purchased by my parents before I was born. The money used to buy it would have been clean. My grandfather was still running the company then and he followed the letter of the law."

"The property will be listed in ninety days. I realize the timeframe may be inconvenient, but we still need to do our due diligence. Once sold, you will receive a portion of the proceeds from the sale," Kirkland explained.

"A portion? Why don't I get the full amount?" Oliver struggled with his temper.

"You received immunity for your crimes. You can't expect to reap the rewards of it. Money will be held out once we determine the upgrades done to the home, when they occurred and the cost. I'm sure that nice media room was a pricey addition," Kirkland said snidely.

Oliver was about to unload, but Harland silenced him. "Remember, son, the government is protecting you. It could just as easily have been five dead bodies on the floor. Someone might still be looking for you."

"Is Mizra going to jail?" Oliver's face brightened at the thought.

"Jay Mizra's fate is none of your business." Kirkland's eyes warned Oliver not to pursue the subject further.

"Fine. Could you tell me then when I can have my parents cremated and interred in the Columbarium at my mother's church? Those were the instructions in the will. I don't think a funeral would be appropriate under the circumstances."

Harland nodded. "I will call today to authorize the cremations. Contact your priest or whomever you wish, and we'll have agents present at the interment for your protection."

"How long will I be here before the US Marshals take me to my new location? Will I still be able to be a financial advisor?" Oliver didn't like being in the dark.

"The US Marshals will contact you later this week to let you know your extraction time. It will likely be several more days before you move. They'll advise if you can get the necessary licenses under your new identity. WITSEC is responsible for finding you a job that fits your skills," Harland explained. "I'll be in touch by Wednesday about the interment date for your parents."

He stood to leave, and Kirkland followed suit, but before he left the room, he got close to Oliver's face. "You better behave, or I'll yank your immunity."

Oliver looked at the table, his fisted hands hidden from view.

***

Oliver grabbed one of his remaining pain pills and a bottle of water from the kitchen. He sat down in the family room with the agents who were on duty. They were barely older than him.

"Hey, I'm going to grab some sub sandwiches for dinner. Do you want one?" Agent Franklin asked Oliver.

"Yeah, that would be great. Thank you. I've got money in my wallet." He started to pull himself up.

"No, man, this is on Uncle Sam. What kind do you want?"

"A meatball sub if they have it."

Franklin nodded and left to get the food.

Agent Garcia turned to Oliver. "Don't let Kirkland get to you. He can be a real jackass."

"So, you heard everything?" Oliver asked, seeing an opening.

"It's hard not to hear Kirkland. Especially when he's posturing." Garcia laughed.

Oliver nodded his agreement and prodded. "I don't know why he got so angry when I asked about Mizra."

"Probably because he had to let Mizra go. He was instrumental in the arrest of the military officer selling our weapons to terrorists."

"Seriously? Is he in WITSEC now?"

"No, but they did give him a new identity. He provided written testimony implicating his father and brother-in-law. He's going to have a hard time hiding from them." Garcia shook his head. "I give him credit for doing the right thing, but I wouldn't want to be in his shoes."

Oliver suppressed a smile. Suddenly, he was in a much better mood.

CHAPTER 33

March 20, 2017

Anna said goodnight to SA Garrett and the other agent babysitting her until the shift change in the morning. Once she was alone in her room, she opened the brown paper bag and quickly hid one of the burner phones in the inside liner of her suitcase, beneath her clothes. She then took the other phone and crawled into bed.

"J.? It's A. They took my phone."

She waited impatiently, worried his phone might have been confiscated, too. After what felt like endless minutes, she received a return text. Her stomach fluttered just knowing Jay was on the other end of the phone.

"I miss you so much, A. I love you."

"Same! They're moving me soon. I bought a couple burner phones, but we need a plan in case they take your phone."

"Once I get my new identity, I'm free. I won't be in witness protection. A, I can find you."

"In case we lose contact with each other we should have a place and a day to meet."

"Let's meet where we planned on going together this summer. Do you remember the hotel?"

"Yes. I'll be there waiting on October 7th. Promise you won't forget me, and you'll be there no matter what happens."

"A., I couldn't forget you if I wanted to, which I don't. I love you and I'm going to marry you someday."

"I love you more than anything, J. Be careful of your family. Don't go back to Dubai. Stay safe."

"I will. Can't wait to see you."

"If I can, I'll call once I'm relocated. If you haven't heard from me, know I'll be waiting at the hotel in October. Now delete these texts!"

Anna heard footsteps coming down the hall, and hid the phone under her pillow. Garrett knocked softly on the door and opened it slowly. Anna pretended to be asleep.

Before she drifted off, she promised herself she'd embrace her new identity. Whatever her new name might be, it would be better than Cahill.

CHAPTER 34

March 22, 2017

Jay was the only civilian passenger on the mid-size private jet. The two pilots were federal agents. They were there to protect Jay and assist the authorities on the ground. As the plane made its final approach to Savannah/Hilton Head International Airport, he saw Lieutenant Benson parked at the side of the runway, waiting.

One of the pilots disengaged the door and lowered the steps for Mizra. As Benson walked over to meet him, Jay extended his hand. It was ignored.

"Where's the money? I want to make this quick."

"Wait here and I'll grab the bags for you." Jay spoke with a calmness he didn't feel.

"No way. For all I know you have FBI agents hiding on that plane waiting to come out and shoot me." Benson drew his gun and motioned for Jay to get back in the plane.

"Why don't you come on up and have a look?" Jay called over his shoulder. "I'll be sure to note your lack of trust in my father and his business associates. Remember, you don't get the other five million dollars until our friends get their weapons."

Benson followed him onto the plane, and Jay pointed to the two black duffels. The lieutenant colonel opened both and examined the contents.

"It seems to all be here. Great doing business with you." Benson put his gun back in its holster and grabbed a bag with each hand.

As he descended the steps, Fulton County sheriff deputies and FBI agents from the Atlanta field office surrounded him.

"Son of a bitch!" he exclaimed as he was pushed face first onto the tarmac and handcuffed.

For his own safety, Jay was led off the plane in handcuffs and placed in an FBI vehicle. Benson was put in another that would bring him back to Fort Stewart for a transfer to the United States Disciplinary Barracks, located at Fort Leavenworth, Kansas.

Once Benson's car was out of sight, Mike got in beside Jay and unlocked his handcuffs.

"You did a great job, Jay."

"What happens now?" He wanted assurance that the government would keep its bargain.

Mike nodded to the jet. "All of your luggage is in the cargo hold, right?" Jay nodded. "Well, once you give me your phone, we can get back on the plane and take you home."

Jay pulled his business phone out of his pocket and handed it over. His private phone was tucked away in his luggage, under the plane.

When he walked back on the plane, he noticed Mike wasn't the only other passenger. US Marshal Walker Grant waited patiently for his new charge to get settled in the seat across from him. He extended his hand to Jay and made his introduction.

Lying on the table between them was a conspicuous manila envelope with "Confidential" stamped on it.

"You do realize I'm not going into the witness protection program?"

"Yes, but you still need a new identity and documents to back it up. That falls under our jurisdiction."

"Do I get to look at it?"

Mike could sense Jay's anticipation.

"After you sign this affidavit." He handed him the folded paper.

Jay felt physically ill as he signed it. He was afraid it would be his death warrant.

"Good luck to you, Jay. I mean that sincerely. You did the right thing." Mike shook Jay's hand and exited the plane.

"Mike isn't coming with us?" Jay asked as he turned to the US Marshal.

Grant continued as if he hadn't even spoken. "Mr. Mizra, even though you are not officially part of the program, I want to see that you are secure. I have a few locations to suggest for you that would be the safest. The choice is yours. The plane will take you back to O'Hare, and then you can decide where you want to go from there."

CHAPTER 35

March 21, 2017

Anna had a visitor. A wave of panic engulfed her when he introduced himself as US Marshal Chris Mulligan.

"Is there someplace private Miss Cahill and I can talk?" he asked McCormack, who directed him to the office, with Anna following behind. The agent gave her shoulder a squeeze of encouragement before she and Mulligan entered the office. Mulligan shut the door behind him to give the two of them privacy.

Anna sat staring at the man who was about to reveal her new life.

"I know this is going to be daunting," he said, "especially for a young woman your age. I want to assure you that I will be right here with you, helping you integrate into your new life. We have managed to secure a diploma for a BA in Political Science in your new name. I realize it must be difficult to leave your university less than two months before you graduate."

"At least I'll have my degree. I'm guessing the US Marshals don't pay tuition for law school," Anna said bleakly.

"I'm afraid not. I did, however, secure a position for you as a paralegal. If you choose to go to law school, the firm may assist you with tuition."

Anna sat quietly for a moment, gathering courage to ask the question she had been anticipating and dreading at the same time. "Where is my new home?"

"Boston, Massachusetts." Mulligan waited patiently for a reaction. He'd assisted dozens of people in the WITSEC program, and he knew that this might not be pretty.

"Wow! That's better than I expected. I thought I'd be out in Idaho or somewhere unpopulated. Will I be able to get my clothes and things from my house? What about my apartment?"

"We've already packed up your apartment. Furniture is not necessary because your new apartment is already furnished. I'll take you to your home to pack some things. Be advised, I will need to go through everything you pack to make sure nothing gives away your real identity. No photos, no clothing with OSU on it, and so on."

Anna nodded gratefully.

"We also need to make a change to your appearance. We have a stylist we use, and she will come here at ten o'clock tomorrow morning. You need a cut and color. Then we will take a picture for your documentation."

"When will I be relocating?"

"Saturday we'll fly to Boston. I can take you to your house now to gather your things."

"What about the FBI agents? I thought no one was supposed to know what I look like or where I'm going except you." Anna heard her nerves creeping back into her voice.

"The two FBI agents have already left. Starting now, I am your only contact. I'm going to ask you to give me your laptop. No one can know where you are going or what your new identity will be. I have a backstory for you to study between now and Saturday. You need to memorize every detail," Mulligan told her sternly.

Again, she nodded her understanding. "Do I get my file now?"

"When we get back from your house. It'll be dark soon. Let's go."

***

"Can I have a few minutes to say goodbye to my home?" Anna asked quietly.

"Sure, take time if you need it," Mulligan said, sympathetic.

He stood outside talking to a local officer while Anna went inside. She entered through the side door so she could avoid passing by the study. She quickly packed her things, leaving behind many treasures. After she'd filled three suitcases, she walked around upstairs. In her mother's room, she opened her jewelry chest and scooped out the diamond and sapphire earrings she loved so much, slipping them in her pocket. She spent some time in the media room and then paused to look at all the photos hung on the hallway wall. Somehow, it seemed like someone else's life.

Mulligan called up to her from the back staircase. She motioned him up and he assisted her in carrying down her bags.

Anna's emotions were flat. She could no longer summon tears for a family she'd never really known.

CHAPTER 36

March 25, 2017

"Emma Miller" walked off the Jetway and into Logan International Airport. Her hair was shoulder length and mahogany red, setting off her blue eyes. It was cloudy and cold as she and Mulligan made their way to the taxi stand. She had been studying her backstory for days and was ready to put it in use.

They went directly from the airport to Anna's new apartment in the Back Bay area of Boston. She felt a rush of excitement when she realized she would be living right in the middle of everything.

The government had furnished the one-bedroom apartment for her. Anna had expected it to be cheaply done and to replace what was there. It was a pleasant surprise that all the furniture was new and suited her taste.

"In good weather, you can walk to your new office from here. Boston Commons is close by and it's a nice area to run in, if you care to do that."

Anna listened to Mulligan's sales pitch as she walked around her new place. When she went into the large bedroom, she found a desk with a laptop sitting on it and a new cell phone.

"You bought me a new computer and phone?"

"Of course. My number is already programmed into it as 'Uncle Chris'. I didn't want to overwhelm you earlier, but one of the caveats of your new job is to get a paralegal certificate. There are many online programs, and you can do the lessons at night and on the weekends. You'll be reimbursed for the cost, of course. Until you complete your certificate, you'll be a legal assistant.

Upon completion, you will be promoted to paralegal and receive a sizeable increase in salary."

"How will I sign up for it?" Anna asked. "I had to give up all my credit cards."

"Follow me back into the family room and we can go over the rest of your packet." Mulligan guided her back to the main room. He placed another manila envelope on the coffee table and proceeded to pull out its contents.

"You already have your driver's license and passport. The WITSEC program has leased a car for you for six months. After that, if you choose to keep it, we will transfer the lease over to you. You're fully insured for those six months. We have a bank account set up for you." He handed her the documentation. "For the next six months you will get the stipend listed directly deposited into your account each month. Any additional expenses need to be run through me. Here are two credit cards in the name of Emma Miller. Anything you charge, unless approved by me, will be up to you to pay from your stipend and your salary."

Anna looked at the stipend and her salary. It was generous, but Boston was an expensive city. "Do I pay my rent from this amount also?"

"The first six months have been paid for in advance. The furniture is yours at no cost to you. We have a team that does an assessment of each location and its average costs. Your stipend, along with what you will be earning at your job, will be more than enough to cover expenses."

"What kind of car and where do I get it?" Anna's curiosity was spilling over.

"Uh..." Mulligan flipped through more paperwork. "Here it is. You have a 2016 silver Toyota Camry. It's parked in your apartment number's designated space in the garage." He handed her a set of keys, then checked his watch. It was three-thirty in the afternoon. "Let's take your car out for a drive and get some groceries for you. Then I'll take you out for a nice dinner to welcome you to Boston." He hesitated for a moment. "Remember, from this moment on, Anna Cahill is dead. You are Emma Miller. Practice calling yourself that in the mirror. I know that sounds strange, but it does help people adjust to their new identity."

"Thank you." Anna's response was genuine. She'd had no idea the program would provide this well for her. "Do you need to check into your hotel first?" she asked.

"I'm a local, which is why I was picked to be your liaison. I live in Braintree, about twenty minutes away, depending on traffic. I meant it when I said I would be here to help you integrate into your new life."

Anna nodded gratefully. She didn't know Mulligan very well, but he seemed to be a nice guy. Over dinner, she learned he had a daughter her age who was about to graduate from Boston University. She began to trust him.

By eight o'clock Saturday night, Anna was alone in her apartment. Her anxiety started to flare, knowing she was all by herself.

She found her medicine bottle and took a pill. Once it started to kick in, she opened her laptop and registered for an online paralegal course. As instructed, she texted the amount she was charged to Mulligan and added a request for refills of her anxiety prescription.

Then she found her burner phone and called Jay. She needed to hear his voice. The phone rang several times and went to voicemail.

She began unpacking to try and take her mind off not being able to reach him. Finally, she crashed a little after one o'clock in the morning, vowing to try Jay again in the morning.

CHAPTER 37

March 27, 2017

US Marshal Peter Olsen sat across the table from Oliver. He explained how the WITSEC program operated and what Oliver could expect over the next several months.

"It's going to be another week before we transport you to your new location. You need to have a post-op with your surgeon, and we need the extra time to obtain the necessary financial licenses."

"What am I supposed to do about a resume? I can't get a job without one."

"We've already secured employment for you at a financial investment firm. You begin April seventeenth. That will give you enough time to completely heal from your wound and adjust to your new surroundings," Olsen reassured him.

"So where am I going and what's my new name?" His nerves were stretched with pain and anticipation.

"I'll give you all the documentation when I come back to pick you up. In the meantime, here is your backstory." Olsen handed him a manila envelope. "You need to memorize every detail before we leave. Don't worry, I'll be at the new location and will check in with you frequently during the first six months. After that, I will be available on an as-needed basis."

"What about my apartment and all my clothes?" Oliver pushed.

"We've already packed up your apartment. I have suitcases for you in my car—the agents are bringing them in now."

Oliver squeezed the incision on his right leg so he could gather some tears. "Mr. Olsen, I need to get in touch with my sister. I said terrible things to her. The counselor at the hospital told me I was experiencing survivor's guilt, but I can't excuse the way I spoke to her. Can you tell me where she is so I can at least write to her and apologize? She's the only family I have left." Oliver's face reflected genuine anguish. It wasn't for his sister. It was the throbbing in his upper leg from the pressure he was applying.

Olsen hesitated. All identities were protected—but Oliver was asking about his sister. Surely he could bend the rules just a little.

He scanned through documents on his laptop and then wrote a name and address on a piece of paper. Oliver thanked him profusely. Now he knew where Anna was living. He was sure Jay would have the same information.

"I'll be in touch." Olsen left and Oliver found himself intrigued by the papers detailing his new life story.

He was desperate to escape his current life, and the one person left in it: Anna.

CHAPTER 38

March 26, 2017

It was a miserable day, inside and out. Anna lay in bed in her new apartment with no motivation at all. Outside it was just above freezing, and rainy. She had one week before she would be Emma Miller full-time.

All at once, she felt desperately lonely. She closed her eyes and tried unsuccessfully to sleep the day away.

She was startled by a phone ringing. Her new phone was by her bed, but it was silent. Anna jumped out of bed and ran toward the sound. In her closet, on a shelf, she found the burner phone.

"Hello?" she said, out of breath.

"Anna?"

When she heard Jay's voice she burst into tears.

"What's wrong? Why are you crying?"

"I can't believe it's you," she answered, trying to quell her tears. "I miss you so much!"

"I don't know that I can wait six months to see you. Anna, tell me where you are and I'll come there," Jay pleaded.

"I'm in Boston, but it's too risky to come now. My handler will be checking in on me regularly for several months."

"Have you spoken to Oliver? Do you know where he was relocated to?"

Through tears, Anna recounted the events of the past two weeks, including the name of her birth mother and Oliver's refusal to give her any information. "He wouldn't even talk to me, and now I won't ever see him again," she finished.

"That's insane! How can he blame you? You're the victim in all this. I hate that you're going through this alone."

"I have you now. As long as we can keep in touch. Have they moved you yet? What happened with the FBI?"

Jay filled Anna in on his participation in the sting to arrest the lieutenant colonel. When he mentioned the affidavit he signed, Anna sucked in her breath.

"Jay, your family will come looking for you! Why would you do that?"

"I didn't have much choice—it was the only way I could get a new identity and documents. Not even the government knows where I am right now. The Marshal assigned to me offered me suggestions on where to live but dropped me off at O'Hare so I could choose in secrecy. Currently, I'm in Houston, Texas, living in a hotel. Honestly, I want to be close to you, so I've been waiting."

Anna was struggling with her desire to see him and her need to keep them both safe. "You could move to New Hampshire. Then we would be driving distance from each other. I've heard Hanover is nice. That's where Dartmouth College is located, so it shouldn't be too isolated for you. We could meet someplace in between for a weekend."

"That would be amazing! I'll pull up listings on my computer. I forgot to ask you what your new name is now."

Anna laughed. "It's Emma Miller, and they dyed my hair a dark red. They also cut it to my shoulders. You might not like me when you see me," she teased.

"I don't care if your hair is green, I still love you. My name is now Leo Samaris. My new backstory says that I'm the product of a British mother and Greek father. This, of course, explains my accent. Passing for Greek is much safer than giving me another Arabic name."

"Let me give you the number of my other burner, in case I have to get rid of one." Anna grabbed the other phone and read off the number.

"I'll call you again Friday evening," he said. "That will give me time to find a place closer to you. I'm not going to wait six months to see you, Anna."

"Agreed. I don't start work until next Monday. I'll look for some nice places between Boston and Hanover where we can meet."

"I love you, Anna."

"I love you, too."

Anna hung up and climbed back under her warm covers, her gray mood now bright. Just the thought of seeing Jay in the next few weeks had lifted her spirits immensely.

The weather forecast for tomorrow would be better than today. She decided she would make the most of it and spend the day shopping for some new work clothes.

CHAPTER 39

March 29, 2017

Jay was booking a flight to Lebanon Municipal Airport, a short drive from Hanover, when his personal phone rang. He assumed it must be Anna.

"It's not even Friday yet," he joked.

"What does Friday have to do with anything?" inquired Mike Mallory.

"How do you have this number and why are you calling me?" Jay went on the defensive; he was supposed to be free.

"I got the number off Anna's cell phone. She called it so much over the past few months, I figured it was you. Smart, having a second phone."

"You still haven't told me why you are calling me," Jay said sharply.

"Look, I'm trying to do you a favor right now. Kirkland, as the US Chief Prosecutor, has issued an extradition request to Dubai. He sent copies of all the evidence with it. Your affidavit was in that package, and your family is now aware of what you did."

Jay panicked. "Shite! It won't be long before they come looking for me."

"They're already hunting for you. An informant told my colleague your father is sending three men to find you. We have their names and flight manifest for their trip to the US. Jay, they will be here tomorrow."

"Where do they land?"

"O'Hare."

"They'll be everywhere. No place is safe because they don't stop until they get what they want!"

"That's the rest of the reason I'm calling. Get rid of your laptop."

"I did before I left Chicago. I have a new one."

"Good! Now, I want you to get rid of your phone—but first write down my number. This is my personal cell. I don't know where you are but that doesn't mean they can't find you. Go buy a couple of burner phones and text me the numbers. Make sure you keep a low profile. I'm going to do right by you, Jay. I know we've put you at great risk."

Jay was shaking but kept his voice steady. "Thank you, Mike. I'll keep in touch." He didn't mention he'd already purchased burner phones. He'd wait a couple of hours and then text him.

In the meantime, he pulled the SIM card out of his phone and cut it up. The phone itself was smashed and thrown in the trash can by the elevator in the hotel lobby.

He finished booking his flight to Hanover. By Friday, he would be in New Hampshire.

Jay wouldn't tell Anna about the threat. He didn't want to frighten her.

CHAPTER 40

March 31, 2017

Anna stepped out onto the sidewalk in front of her building. It was barely above freezing, but she needed to run to clear her head before she started her full-time life as Emma Miller. She was dressed in thick leggings, with a long-sleeved shirt, fleece pullover and a knit beanie pulled down over her ears. Her destination was Boston Commons. She had taken Mulligan's advice and found it a perfect spot for running.

She jogged in place, waiting for the light at a crosswalk to change. A loud screech made her step back. A blacked-out van stood in front of her, blocking her way. Before she could scream, the door slid open and four strong arms grabbed her, lifted her inside and slid the door shut.

As the van sped away, Anna screamed and fought, but one of the men pressed his weight down over her upper body to hold her still. She felt a needle enter her arm. A warmth spread through her veins, and she slipped into unconsciousness.

***

"They took her! How did they find her?" Jay's voice was loud in Mike Mallory's ear.

"What? Hold on. Let me get to a quiet place." Mike motioned for Kate to follow him into the closest conference room.

Kate, seeing the look on his face, brought a pad and pen. Something was very wrong.

"Ok, I have you on speakerphone. SA DeSoto is with me. Can you start again?"

"Anna was abducted. I don't know how my father's men found her, but they did. I know the type of men my father employs for his dirty work. They will hurt her just to punish me! Someone on your side gave up her identity and address," Jay's anger boiled over.

"Let's step back a moment. How do you know these men have Anna?"

"Because they called me and gave me twenty-four hours to exchange myself for her freedom. These men will torture and kill her in front of me just to hurt me. Then they'll murder me. You promised you would help me!"

Mike's face lost all color. There was another mole in the US Marshals. That was the only way to explain it.

"Jay, do you know where Anna is located?"

"She's in Boston, but I don't know where they are holding her yet. I'm supposed to text them when I get there, and they'll give me the address. I was about to get on a flight from Houston headed to Hanover, New Hampshire, when I got the call. I just changed my ticket, so I'll be in Boston by three o'clock this afternoon. What are you going to do?" Jay was on the verge of breaking down. Someone had risked Anna's safety, and now her life was in danger.

Kate made notes furiously on her pad, turning it so Mike could read them. She was going to step out and call Chris Mulligan, Anna's handler, and get to the bottom of this leak. Mike nodded and continued.

"Jay, Kate just left to track down the source of the leak. She and I will be on the next flight to Boston. I'll contact the FBI field office there for backup. Has she been in contact with Oliver?"

"No. She doesn't even know where he is right now. After his last exchange with her, I'm not sure she wants to know. Do you think it was him who contacted my father?"

"I think it's a good possibility. He has a strong dislike for you and if he knew you were free, that would give him motive. We are two and a half hours away from Boston by plane. It's possible we will land around the same time as you. I'll text you the flight information as soon as I have it. Wait for us before texting the kidnappers. If we have any hope of getting Anna back unharmed, we need to take a little time and get this extraction set up properly."

"Do you know what they can do to her in that amount of time?" Jay's throat was thick with tears.

"Try not to think about it. I know that's a shit answer, but we only have one chance to get this right. You said they would torture her to hurt you. Let's assume they won't hurt her until you are there to see it. By then, we will have a team ready to get her out safely."

"Find the bastard who contacted my father. I'll meet your flight in Boston." Jay hung up.

Mike left the conference room in search of Kate. She was at her desk, on the phone. She held up one finger to Mike, indicating he needed to wait. "Ok, we'll deal with the security breach later. In the meantime, get Oliver into custody."

Mike's face began turning red when he heard Oliver's name. Kate quickly filled him in.

"Chris Mulligan never gave Anna's location to anyone. He's a seasoned marshal and is incredibly upset to hear what's happened. He gave me the name of Oliver's handler, Peter Olsen. When I called him, he admitted giving Oliver his sister's new information. Cahill played on his sympathies to get it, and Olsen knows he just sank his career. Still, he's willing to do whatever he can to assist us. You heard me tell him to pick Oliver up immediately. Peter will check his phone for any calls to Dubai."

"Good work. Now book us two seats on the next flight to Boston. I'm going to get Harland up to speed and ask him to rally the Boston FBI to give us a team."

CHAPTER 41

March 31, 2017

Anna's head felt like it was being stabbed with ice picks. She struggled to open her eyes. When she did, she realized she was lying on a sofa in a small but tidy home. As she sat up, she cried out in pain.

"Finally, you are awake," a voice behind her said. Her mind was reeling, but she immediately identified a thick Arab accent. The man moved around and stood in front of her. He handed her a bottle of water. "You have medicine for your headache in there." He motioned to her purse, lying on the floor next to the sofa.

"Yes, I know." She was irritated by pain, the fact she couldn't remember what happened and that he had gone through her things. "Who are you and how did I get wherever this is?" Anna was frightened but she also had a migraine. The discomfort set the tone of her voice.

The man laughed at her annoyance, pulled up a chair and sat in front of her. "My name is Zayan. You don't remember anything because the medication we used to sedate you affects your short-term memory. You were being difficult so we may have overdosed you a bit."

Anna couldn't wrap her head around what he was saying. "Why would you abduct me? I don't even know who you are or where you're from."

"I, along with my associates, Irfan and Nazif"—he made a wide gesture toward two men standing in the doorway to the kitchen—"are from Dubai. We have been tasked by Hadiq al-Mizra to find his son and execute him."

Anna's face lost all color, but still she said, "Why would you kidnap me? I don't know anything."

"Maybe not, but we have it on good authority you are Jahir's girlfriend. We've already called him to let him know we have you. He's aware we'll torture you unless he shows up to save you." Zayan smiled, and the other men laughed.

"How do you have his phone number?"

"Ah, that is all thanks to you. It's the only number you've called on your cell phone. We took a chance and called it. Sure enough, Jahir answered, and he is quite concerned about you."

Anna couldn't believe this was happening. She was supposed to be under government protection. "How did you find me?"

"So many questions!" Zayan leaned forward until he was six inches from Anna's face. "Apparently, your brother doesn't like you much. To be truthful, we didn't know where to start until he called Mr. Mizra with your identity and location."

Anna couldn't hide her shock. "Oliver told you where I was? How would he even know?"

"What difference does it make? We have you now, and soon we will have Jahir."

"I need to use the restroom," Anna demanded. She wasn't bound in any way, so she assumed the men were armed.

Zayan motioned to Nazif, a man in his early thirties with an M-9 strapped to his hip. "Escort Ms. Cahill to the bathroom."

Anna was a little wobbly when she stood up but soon gained her balance and followed Nazif. He stood outside the door until she finished. Looking around as she walked back to the family room, she peered through the sheer curtains across the window. The house next door was very close. She made a guess that she was in a row house in a middle-class neighborhood. From the flooring and wallpaper, she surmised it was built in the 1970s and not much had been done to it since.

Zayan was no longer in sight, but Irfan, the third of her kidnappers, was standing by the sofa, directing her to sit. She obliged.

Zayan returned from the kitchen. "It appears we have several hours before Jahir will arrive. Do you know where he is coming from?" he asked Anna.

"I have no idea. Even if I did, I wouldn't tell you," she said with more boldness than she felt.

"Well, we don't want you to be bored." He approached her with a syringe. She tried to jump up, but Nazif and Irfan were faster and they held her down.

She fought and screamed, but within moments of feeling the warm liquid enter her veins, she was unconscious.

CHAPTER 42

March 31, 2017

Oliver was stretched out in a recliner, memorizing his backstory. He had been informed Olsen would be coming in a few days with all the documents for his new identity and to take him to his new home.

The front door opened and closed, but Oliver ignored it. He had become accustomed to the agents coming and going from the house.

"Mr. Cahill, please stand up."

Oliver looked up to see Peter Olsen and another US Marshal standing a few feet in front of him.

"You got the documentation early?" he asked as he stood up. "Give me ten minutes to pack my stuff."

"You're not going to your new location, Oliver. My colleague, Dan Castro, and I are taking you into custody." Olsen motioned for Castro to grab Oliver's cell phone off the end table.

"What the hell is going on? What do you mean you're taking me into custody? I have full immunity." Oliver was irate. He looked to his left, where Castro was going through his phone.

"We got it, sir." Castro nodded to Olsen.

"Got what?" Oliver took a step toward Olsen, only for one of the agents on duty to grab his arm and turn him around. A zip tie tightened around his wrists.

"Mr. Cahill, according to your phone history, you have made a few calls to Dubai. We're going to make you comfortable in one of our holding cells until we see if the number traces back to Hadiq al-Mizra."

"What? Why do you think I would call him and risk my deal with the government?"

"I'd wonder that myself, if I didn't know that your sister, Anna, was kidnapped this morning by Hadiq's men. Let's go."

Olsen motioned to the agent and Castro. They pushed Oliver into the back seat of a black SUV and secured his feet with another zip tie.

"Dan here will ride in the back with you," Olsen said. "He has a notoriously short temper, so I'd behave if I were you."

Castro held his gun to Oliver's ribs. "Let's hope we don't hit any speed bumps." He smirked.

"I want to speak to my lawyer immediately," Oliver demanded.

"Don't worry. It's a short ride and we'll give him a call when we arrive. In the meantime, picture your innocent sister being tortured as we speak." Olsen's voice dripped with acid. He was furious with himself for being duped.

Oliver leaned his head against the window of the back seat and felt a pang of remorse. He hadn't thought about Anna being hurt. He'd just wanted to offer up Jahir to his father, and his sister to be the bait.

CHAPTER 43

March 31, 2017

A dozen agents and one civilian, Jay Mizra, gathered around the conference table at the FBI field office in Boston.

Mike Mallory stood up in front of a smartboard. He pointed to the photograph on the screen. "We believe this is the house where al-Mizra's men are holding Anna Cahill captive. They used Anna's cell phone to call Jay Mizra; we were able to triangulate the number with a cell tower to narrow down the location. According to property records in the area, this is the one house that is owned by a foreign national from Dubai."

Jay shifted nervously as Mike continued his presentation. He drew directly on the picture where all the agents would be positioned, ready to enter the house. Due to the proximity of the other homes, they would have to wait until dark and quietly evacuate the closest neighbors. Jay had made it clear that his father's men would not hesitate to fire at will and didn't care about any incidental casualties.

Jay looked at his watch. It was five-thirty. It would be two more hours before nightfall. He was terrified of what they would do with Anna in the meantime.

His phone began to ring. Everyone fell silent when he informed them it was his father's men. He put the call on speaker. "Hello?"

"Jahir, we are getting restless waiting for you. I don't think your girlfriend appreciates your tardiness."

"You better not touch her!"

Zayan let out a cruel laugh. "I suggest you get here soon and alone, or she may not be available to see you."

Mike nodded to Jay. They had rehearsed this phone call.

"My connection was delayed. I land at Logan Airport at twenty past seven. I'll arrive before eight o'clock. Text me the address."

"Call me when you get to Boston, and I'll send it. We'll be waiting for you," Zayan replied, and the phone disconnected.

Jay looked directly at Mike. "They will hurt her." He was restless and frustrated. Anna needed him.

"Patience, ok? We are under the assumption they won't do anything to her until you're there to witness it."

Jay fell silent, but his face was riddled with concern.

"Ok," Mike continued to the group at large. "I want the neighbors moved to safety and everyone in their positions at seven-forty-five. Once Jay enters the house, the three kidnappers will be focused on him. Remember, they will be armed and won't hesitate to shoot. SA DeSoto and I will be near the front door, hidden from view but ready to enter. I want the other five teams in their positions. Teams two and three will cover the back door and the basement doors. Teams four and five will cover the windows on either side of the house. Team six, your job will be to keep the civilians quiet and safe over here." Mike motioned to an alleyway two hundred yards from the house. "We'll be on comms. If anyone can get a visual inside the home, let everyone know. Be ready to enter on my signal. Any questions?"

"Should we have an ambulance out of sight but standing by, in case Anna needs medical attention?" Kate was as worried as Jay but keeping calm.

"Yes, would you take care of it?" Mike asked. "Make sure no lights or sirens. They should be positioned a block away from the target. Alright, grab a sandwich and be ready to roll out in ninety minutes."

The Boston field agents filed out of the conference room, leaving Mike, Kate and Jay.

"What happens after we recover Anna?" Jay asked. "She can't go back into WITSEC. She'll need a whole new identity. I will too for that matter." They needed an exit strategy.

Kate tried to reassure him. "Don't worry, Jay. The US Marshal who placed Anna here is working on new documents for her and for you as well. Given the breach in the agency's protocol and subsequent consequences, I don't think the US Marshals will argue with you two going off-grid."

Mike and Kate urged Jay to come eat with them, but he refused. He spent the remaining time pacing the conference room, terrified of what might be happening to Anna.

CHAPTER 44

March 31, 2017

Anna struggled out of her drug-induced sleep. Something felt different. She was no longer lying on the sofa, but instead sitting in a chair with her hands zip-tied to the arms and her feet bound together on the floor. She was positioned in the middle of the family room, facing the front door.

As she shook off the fog, she realized she had been asleep for several hours. The once bright house was now darkened, with only two dim lamps on the end tables. The heavier drapes had been drawn, leaving only a few inches of the windows exposed, presumably to watch for Jay. Even the kitchen light was extinguished.

"What the hell did you give me?" Anna growled at Zayan, who was standing in front of her.

"A generous dose of Versed. Don't worry, the dizziness and any headache will wear off shortly." He smiled at her.

"Why did you tie me up? I've been unconscious the whole time!"

Irfan, who couldn't have been more than twenty years old, walked up alongside her with an AR-15 slung around his shoulder. "Your boyfriend is going to be here very soon. He needs to understand the gravity of your situation."

"What are you talking about?" Anna looked from Irfan to Zayan. The latter was holding a 9mm gun in his hand. He kept it there as he smacked her across the face. She immediately tasted blood.

"It's nothing personal, Ms. Cahill," he said. "Jahir needs to understand the consequences of his actions."

"So you hit me?" Anna was incredulous.

"What hurts more? When you're injured or someone you love is?" Zayan waxed philosophical.

Nazif moved out from behind her to where she could see him and the M9 tucked in his waistband. He looked at Zayan, who nodded. With a loud grunt and using all his weight, Nazif backhanded her with a closed fist across the right side of her face.

Anna's head was lolling about, semi-conscious. Her face was bloody, and swelling had begun around her eyes and cheekbones.

Satisfied with the initial damage, the three men took up positions in a semicircle around her. The safety was removed from each weapon.

***

Outside, the FBI agents moved silently, taking the assigned positions around the house. Mike bent down on the front porch and peered through the opening in the drapes. He could see all three men surrounding Anna, who appeared unconscious in the center of the room.

He moved away from the window and whispered into his comm, "Team two, are you in place at the back door?"

"Yes," came the response. "We can enter directly into the kitchen. We have eyes on the perps and Anna."

"Good. Once Jay enters and has their attention, kick in the back door with weapons ready. DeSoto and I will enter through the front door. Hadiq's men all have bulletproof vests. If they raise a weapon, fire at will, but strategically."

The agents confirmed the order. They would be aiming for the lower extremities to take them down.

Mike nodded to Jay, who knocked on the door.

"Who is it?" Zayan asked loudly. He smiled to his cohorts and tightened his grip on his gun.

"You know it's Jahir," Jay said tensely. "I'm going to enter. I'm unarmed."

Jay was wearing a bulletproof vest under his jacket, but his heart still raced. He opened the door and his breath caught when he saw Anna tied up with her head hanging down.

"Jahir, see what happens when you keep us waiting?" Zayan lifted Anna's head up by her hair.

Rage overflowed from Jay at the sight of Anna injured. He moved toward her captors. They raised their weapons, stopping him mid-step.

A loud crack of wood breaking caused the men to turn around in time to see teams two and three rushing in with weapons drawn.

"Put down your weapons or we'll shoot," advised the first agent.

Nazif and Irfan looked at Zayan, who was pointing his gun at Jay.

"If you shoot, Jahir dies and so does Anna," he told the agents.

That was Mike's cue. He and Kate rushed in from the front with their weapons ready to fire. The kidnappers were now surrounded by six FBI agents. Zayan squeezed the trigger and fired at Jay. Gunshots rang out from all around as Jay fell to the ground.

By the time teams four and five rushed in, all three of al-Mizra's men were on the ground, bleeding. Only Zayan had sustained a mortal wound, a gunshot to the forehead. The agents handcuffed Nazif and Irfan, who were groaning loudly in pain.

Mike radioed for the ambulance down the block to come immediately and requested two more be dispatched. Kate ran over to Jay. The vest had saved his life, but his chest felt like it was burning. When he looked at where the bullet had entered the vest, he felt faint; it was an inch from his heart.

Mike ran to cut Anna's ties. He picked her up out of the chair and she fell against him. He gently laid her on the floor as the lights of the ambulance cast a red glow in the darkened room. A quick survey of the agents assured Mike that none of his people were injured.

The EMTs loaded Anna into the ambulance. Jay insisted on riding with her. Mike agreed on the condition that he get an X-ray to see if any ribs had been cracked by the bullet he took.

Nazif and Irfan had both suffered multiple wounds to their legs. They were loaded, still restrained, into the next ambulances. Two agents rode along in each ambulance, while Kate and Mike followed Anna's to the hospital. Team six brought the neighbors back to their homes, and the remaining agents were left to secure the scene and wait for the coroner.

CHAPTER 45

April 5, 2017

Anna and Jay sat side by side on the sofa in the hotel suite, holding hands. They were anxiously awaiting the arrival of Chris Mulligan with their new documentation. Anna's swelling had subsided, and the cut above her left eye, from the barrel of the 9mm, was covered with steri-strips. With a little extra makeup, she could hide what was left of the bruising. She would be able to go to the airport without garnering odd looks.

Mulligan had been kind enough to send a hairdresser to the hotel to change her look, again. She now had strawberry blonde hair cut in a pert bob to her chin. It suited her much more than the dark red. Jay had made the only significant change he could; he shaved off his goatee.

A knock on the door had Jay jumping to his feet to answer. Mulligan entered with a smile and two manila envelopes.

"You each have a complete set of documents, and I made sure they aren't entered in our database. From this point on, you're ghosts. Are you certain this is what you want? We can't offer protection if we don't have your information."

"Thank you, Chris. For everything," said Anna. "I think Jay and I would both feel safer if no one could track us."

"Has Oliver been charged yet?" Jay asked.

Mulligan frowned and looked down. "I'm afraid not. His attorney tore holes in our investigation to the point where the chief federal prosecutor didn't feel there was enough evidence to make a charge stick."

"How is that possible?" Anna was furious. "He gave confidential information to Jay's father, who wanted Jay dead and me as collateral damage!"

"I agree, but the US Marshals who brought him in searched his phone without a warrant, making the phone calls to Mr. Mizra inadmissible. Even if the federal prosecutor was able to get the phone records admitted, there is no proof Oliver gave out Anna's WITSEC information." Mulligan sighed deeply.

"So he's roaming around?" Anna pressed.

"He's been given his new identity and moved to a new location. This way, we can keep an eye on him. The federal government is trying to extradite Hadiq and Parishad based on what happened, but there are no guarantees."

"Thank you, Chris. We appreciate you getting this done so quickly for us." Jay shook his hand.

Anna gave him a quick hug.

"Be careful, ok?" Mulligan looked like a worried father.

They both nodded, and once he was out the door, they opened their envelopes and checked their new identities.

Jay opened his laptop and booked the next flight out. While he worked on their flights and hotel reservations, Anna dug through her backpack until she found what she needed, placing it in her purse.

"I'll be right back. I need to mail something. Do you want me to grab some snacks for the flight?" Anna lingered by the door.

"We're flying first class, so no snacks needed. What could you possibly have to mail?" Jay asked, looking up from his laptop.

"I want to send a small thank you to Kate and Mike. They treated me so well during all of this." Anna smiled.

"You are very thoughtful, but don't take too long. We're going to be on a flight in four hours. We're leaving the country tonight!"

A block from the hotel, Anna found a FedEx store. She had the portable hard drive, secured in bubble wrap, and a letter packed into a small box, addressed to Mike Mallory at the Chicago field office. Because they would be out of the country tonight, she had the package shipped two-day air.

When Anna returned fifteen minutes later, Jay had the suitcases open on the bed and was busy packing.

"Our flight is in a little over three hours," he said with a smile. "You'd better start packing."

"I'm so excited!" She kissed him on the cheek and began to pack her bags.

Jay sat on the bed and motioned for her to sit beside him for a moment.

"Anna, I want you to know that I have over twenty million dollars in a Swiss bank account. What's mine is yours. We won't have to worry about money in our new life. To prove it to you, here's my bank and account number." He handed her a small card. Anna tucked it away in her backpack next to the folded paper with her mother's account information.

"Well, I should probably tell you that I also have a Swiss bank account and it has a little over sixteen million dollars in it." She laughed at the shocked expression on Jay's face.

"Where did you get that kind of money? I know your father left you out of your parents' will."

Anna explained to Jay how she'd happened to become independently wealthy. He was shocked but happy.

"Your mom really did love you," he said as he pulled her into a hug.

"I know she did. She was a wonderful mother." Anna laid her head on his shoulder for a few minutes. "Ok, the past is past. We need to get moving and get out of here!"

They were checked out of the hotel within the hour and on their way to Logan International Airport.

CHAPTER 46

April 5–6, 2017

Anna sank back into her first-class seat as the plane took off for Barcelona. For the first time in weeks, she felt relaxed and safe. She and Jay had used their new passports at Logan International, and no one batted an eye.

She held Jay's hand and admired his clean-shaven look.

"You look more handsome without the goatee."

"I like you as a strawberry blonde. It suits you." Jay smiled as he leaned over and kissed her.

They would land in Barcelona at noon, local time, and then take a private car to their hotel in Andorra la Vella. Jay had booked them into the Grand Plaza Hotel & Wellness, under his new name, for a couple weeks while they looked around Andorra and chose an apartment to rent. It felt safer renting for a while. Jay was already fluent in French and Spanish, so Anna promised to learn Catalan. Between the two of them, they would be able to communicate with anyone.

After an eight-hour flight, Eve "Evie" Sanders and Lucas "Luke" Mantzos deplaned in Barcelona. The drive to Andorra was a little over an hour. Even though it was the afternoon, they were exhausted. Jay decided he was too hungry to sleep. After settling into their spacious suite, he ordered a bottle of pinot grigio from room service to be sent up along with two orders of pappardelle with lobster.

Despite Jay's desire to conserve water, Anna insisted they take separate showers so as not to miss room service. She showered first then turned the bathroom over to Jay.

Within a few minutes, there was a knock at the door and the waiter set up their meal at the dining table. He opened the wine for Anna, and she tasted it. It was sublime. She nodded and the waiter poured her a full glass and promptly left. Anna called Jay through the bathroom door and then sat at the table with her wine, waiting for him. He soon joined her, and they toasted to their new life together.

After their meal and two glasses of wine for Jay, they were ready to get some sleep. Anna closed the blackout curtains to keep out the midday sun. They snuggled together, and soon Jay was snoring.

CHAPTER 47

April 7, 2017

Mike returned from lunch to find a FedEx package on his desk, and Kate waiting for him.

"I've been dying for you to get back," she enthused. "It arrived right after you left, shipped from Boston. It must be something from Jay or Anna."

Mike opened the box and removed a three-inch-by-four-inch portable hard drive. Kate noticed the letter and read it aloud:

"*Thank you both for everything you did to protect me. I discovered this on my final visit to my family home. Watch the video on the external hard drive and make sure you have the volume on high. Justice needs to be done. Sincerely, A.*"

Mike grabbed his laptop and the drive. Kate was on his heels as they entered the conference room. She closed the door behind them and sat next to him, impatiently waiting as he turned his computer on and plugged in the drive. He quickly found the video dated March 10, 2017. With the volume turned up, they fixed their eyes on what was unfolding in front of them:

Oliver and Al Barakat entered the foyer of the Cahill home and proceeded to the study where Thomas, Meredith and David were waiting.

"What the hell is this all about? Who are you to call us out here in the middle of a workday?" Thomas' voice boomed.

"We seem to have a problem, Dad. Someone leaked information to the FBI that Cahill Investments is involved in illegal transactions with foreign nationals."

"And you think it was one of us?" David asked in disbelief.

"It doesn't really matter who it was. What matters is the chain reaction it caused. Al, would you like to explain, since you are here at Jahir Mizra's request?" Oliver was preening with authority.

"The investigation into Cahill and Jahir Mizra caused a US military officer to cancel the delivery of guns to Hamas. Guns that Hadiq ibn Khalid al-Mizra has already promised."

"What does an illegal arms deal have to do with Cahill Investments?" Meredith was confused.

"C'mon, Mom," Oliver said. "If the FBI stops its investigation into our company, the heat will be off the arms dealer and the Mizras can complete their deal."

"How in fuck's name are we supposed to stop an FBI investigation we knew nothing about?" Thomas took a menacing step toward Al, who also took a step forward.

Al grabbed the gun from the waistband of his pants and pointed it at Thomas Cahill.

"What? No! Oliver, stop him!" Meredith cried, but it was too late.

Al put a bullet in Thomas' stomach, and he hit the floor. Meredith dropped to her knees beside him.

"Oliver, you're helping him! Why would you do this?" David asked, backing up against the desk.

Without hesitation, Al put two bullets into his chest. Meredith looked up at her son, screaming. Al put a bullet in her forehead and turned to Oliver.

"Don't point that thing at me! What the hell is wrong with you? I did everything Jay asked me to; you got your money."

"Jay's orders came directly from Mr. Mizra Senior, and he doesn't like loose ends," Al sneered.

Oliver pounced on him and they wrestled to the ground. It was hard for Mike and Kate to see who had the gun during the scuffle. Then the sound of two bullets, almost simultaneous, rang out.

Oliver pushed Al off him, giving the camera a view of Barakat's stomach wound. Oliver's upper right thigh was hemorrhaging blood. He pulled his cell phone out of his pocket and started to dial before he passed out.

***

Mike and Kate sat back in horror. Oliver had played them from the beginning; Jay and his father had ordered the murders of everyone, including Oliver. No wonder he hated Jay so much—he'd been double-crossed.

"What would Oliver gain by betraying his family?" Kate asked, staring at the screen in shock.

"If I had to guess, I'd wager he was clearing the path for himself at Cahill Investments and establishing a business partnership with the Mizras for arms dealing." Mike shook his head. "Let's call the US Marshals' office. We'll give Chris Mulligan the honor of picking up Oliver and bringing him here. His attorney can't get him out of this." He sighed in disgust.

"So, Anna found this video right before she went into WITSEC. Why wouldn't she have told us sooner?"

"I think she was scared and trying to protect herself," Mike surmised. "More importantly, if she watched this, she knows Jay is complicit. Who knows where they are right now?"

"She's all alone with Jay. What do you think she's going to do?" Kate was afraid.

"Hopefully, she's going to call us with their location, and we can pick him up. With this evidence, the UAE will have to extradite Jay's father and brother-in-law."

"What about pressing charges against her for withholding evidence?" Kate asked.

"I don't think we'll ever find her," Mike replied. "Even if we did, I'd say she's suffered enough."

CHAPTER 48

April 8, 2017

Oliver was lying poolside at his new apartment complex, gaining attention from several promising women on the other side of the pool. He stood up to dive in, swim over and introduce himself, the brand-new Max Crawford.

He had only taken two steps toward the pool when the US Marshals and FBI agents swooped in very publicly, pushed him to the ground and arrested him for multiple counts of first-degree murder.

"Can I at least put my shoes and shirt on?" Oliver was caustic.

Chris Mulligan heard Oliver complaining as he walked across the parking lot to greet his new charge. "Don't worry, Mr. Cahill, we've got something for you to put on."

The agents put him in the back of a van and provided him with a plain T-shirt, joggers and slip-on sneakers. He was escorted first onto the plane, listening to the flight crew chatter about a prisoner being onboard. Mulligan put him by the window in the last row of seats and sat next to him, his hand never far from his firearm. A second US Marshal was seated across the aisle.

Mulligan pulled a sweatshirt out of his carry-on bag and handed it to Oliver. "You might want to put this on when we get back to Chicago. Oh, I see you are tied up and can't put it on. Well, me and the other Marshal"—he pointed to his colleague— "and about half a dozen FBI agents will be at O'Hare Airport to make sure you are dressed warmly."

It was mid-afternoon in Chicago when Mulligan and his partner walked Oliver off the plane. They waited for every other passenger to exit before shoving him into the aisle. As promised, half a dozen agents were at the gate. They had several cars lined up in a caravan.

As they steered Oliver to the center car, there was a loud noise. The agents drew their guns, some ushering people back inside the airport and some ducking around cars, looking for the sniper. Mike Mallory looked down, and then called the agents back.

Oliver Cahill was shot dead, right between the eyes.

CHAPTER 49

April 6, 2017

The sun was setting. Anna finished applying her makeup and dressed casually in jeans, a blue sweater, a beige peacoat and her running shoes. She gathered her suitcases and rolled them all to the door.

She took one last look at Jay, sleeping soundly, and silently congratulated herself on putting GHB in the wine bottle.

As she stepped out of the elevator in the lobby, she bumped into a dark-haired man just under six feet, dropping her key card. She picked it up and handed it to him. "Pardon me, sir, I believe you'll need this," she said with a smile and proceeded through the lobby without looking back.

She got into a waiting car and made the return drive to Barcelona airport. She was all alone, a ghost, but she wouldn't have it any other way.

Anna reached into her purse and pulled out the card Jay had given her. On it was the name of a Swiss bank with his account number written on the back. She now had over thirty-six million, untraceable dollars.

She knew the FBI would never pursue her. Anna had given them a parting gift they couldn't refuse. She was completely free, and a very wealthy young woman.

At the airport, she stood in front of the departure screens, excited at all the possibilities. She felt giddy as she chose her new destination and strode to the counter to buy her ticket. She was exactly who she wanted to be: Evie Sanders, an orphaned heiress.

AUTHOR PROFILE

Shannon Condon, an award-winning author, has been writing since her early teens. She graduated Phi Kappa Phi from the College of Journalism and Communications at the University of Florida. In 2014, she seized the opportunity to become a full-time author, resulting in the creation of the *Magdalena* series. This gripping series follows the journey of protagonist Maggie Curran from a newly orphaned fifteen-year-old to an adult with a family and a career as a black ops assassin.

Shannon's passion lies in crafting suspenseful thrillers and crime mysteries, keeping readers on the edge of their seats with unexpected twists and turns. *When Anna Came Home* is her new standalone crime thriller which is written in her signature style: fast-paced, twisty, and it will keep you guessing until the end. Shannon's dedication to authenticity takes her to the locations where her books are set, allowing her to immerse herself in the culture and bring genuine details to her settings.

Shannon has lived in different parts of the country but has called North Carolina home for the past twenty years. Watching her sons pursue their dreams serves as a constant inspiration for her.

Instagram: Shannon Condon (@shannoncondonauthor)

Threads: @shannoncondonauthor

Goodreads: https://www.goodreads.com/shannoncondon

Amazon: rb.gy/4ccysk

Website: https://shannoncondonauthor.com

WHAT DID YOU THINK OF
WHEN ANNA CAME HOME?

A big thank you for purchasing this book. It means a lot that you chose this book specifically from such a wide range on offer. I do hope you enjoyed it.

Book reviews are incredibly important for an author. All feedback helps them improve their writing for future projects and for developing this edition. If you are able to spare a few minutes to post a review on Amazon, that would be much appreciated.

PUBLISHER INFORMATION

Rowanvale Books provides publishing services to independent authors, writers and poets all over the globe. We deliver a personal, honest and efficient service that allows authors to see their work published, while remaining in control of the process and retaining their creativity. By making publishing services available to authors in a cost-effective and ethical way, we at Rowanvale Books hope to ensure that the local, national and international community benefits from a steady stream of good quality literature.

For more information about us, our authors or our publications, please get in touch.

www.rowanvalebooks.com
info@rowanvalebooks.com

www.ingramcontent.com/pod-product-compliance
Lightning Source LLC
Chambersburg PA
CBHW031431250626

47155CB00004B/1698
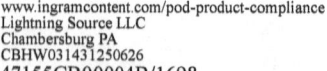